Man to Man Coverage

Rangers Football
Book 6

Kameron Claire

Snuggle Whore Press, LLC

To all the Witty, Wicked & Wild Readers...
Never let them silence our Witty tongues,
Never let them shame our Wicked needs,
Never let them stop our Wild deeds.

Thank you for the love and support!

ROCKY MOUNTAIN
RANGERS

Prologue

"I say we invite that one and that one and, of course, the redhead over there back to our hotel."

Rex shakes his head. "Coach will have our ass if he finds out we brought a bunch of strippers home with us."

"Dancers—" Jepson flashes a brunette his Sunday school smile "—and the coach isn't invited."

"Dancers, whatever," Rex rolls his eyes.

"Which one do you like, Jaxson?"

Jaxson shrugs and tosses back what's left of his beer. "I don't care."

"Sure you do. You want the redhead, don't you?" Jepson taunts. "He always goes for the redhead."

Jaxson rolls his eyes. "Actually, I was digging the blonde."

"I already called dibs on the blonde," Jepson smirks, his eye contact hard across the table at his brother.

"Of course you did," Jaxson mutters.

The blonde in question comes up and flashes the

table a big smile. "Anyone looking for a lap dance?"

"Actually, honey, we were hoping for something a bit more intimate," Jepson leans forward.

She tsks and throws him a placating smile. "I'm sure you are, but this is not that kind of establishment."

"I'm sure for the right price it could be any kind of establishment we want."

"Where are you boys from?"

"Spring City, Colorado. What about you?"

"I'm Nashville, born and raised, sugar."

Jepson lets his eyes trail down her body. "What time do you get off work?"

"Why?" She straightens, putting more distance between her and him.

"The boys would love to see Music Row. Since you are homegrown, you could show us all the places only the locals go."

"Every place on Music Row is good, and they are easy to find. Just walk a straight line and follow your nose or your ears, depending upon what you are looking for."

"But don't you want to entertain a couple of big badass football players?"

Plastering on a sweet smile, she bats her eyelashes. "My boyfriend is a big badass football player."

"From Nashville?" Rex arches his brow.

"You damn right," she replies.

"Yeah, but Nashville sucks," Jepson chuckles. "We're going to be National Champions this year, honey. Wouldn't you like to suck the dick of a winner at least once this year?"

Her smile fades, and she turns to walk away. Jepson reaches out and grabs her hand—the one thing you're not allowed to do.

"Man, don't touch the dancers," Rylie says, putting his drink down. He looks over his shoulder at security, which is walking their way. "We're not in Denver, and the women here don't know you like that, so keep your hands to yourself."

"Fuck you, choirboy." Jepson releases her hand and puts his hands in his lap. "Sorry, honey. I just wanted to apologize. I didn't mean to infer you'll be sucking my dick. It could be one of my teammates."

She looks over our heads and shakes her head, letting the security guard know it's okay for the moment. "You're an asshole."

Jepson smiles. "Yeah, but I'm a hot asshole."

She rolls her eyes and walks away at about the same time a waitress walks up with another round of drinks. We are not supposed to be drinking tonight, and yet Jepson's on his third whiskey on the rocks. His twin brother Jaxson is nursing his beer, and Devlin, Rylie and Rex are drinking Diet Coke.

"We should get out of here and check out a couple of local artists on our walk back to the hotel," Devlin says, throwing down a twenty and standing, brokering no questions that he's leaving. Rylie also stands, throwing down his own Jackson, following Devlin out.

Rex rubs the back of his neck. "What do you guys think?"

Prologue Continued...
Rex

Fucking Jepson. He's one of my best friends, but sometimes the shit he pulls stinks a little too badly and lingers a bit too long. In less than sixty seconds, his shirt is torn and his back is scratched by a stripper's acrylic nails that had to be filed to vampiric points to make those marks and he's bitching at his twin who has a red welt on his cheek that will be black by the morning.

The Uber driver stops in front of our hotel, and suddenly I need a breather from these two. I treasure their friendship, but I'm glad I'm not related. We get out and I drop back as the two of them enter the lobby, sneaking around to the side of the building before they realize I'm gone. Broadway Street is two blocks away, and I should have enough time to listen to the next up-and-coming country star sing a couple of songs before curfew.

I pass a brightly lit tourist trap stuffed with souvenirs and knickknacks, bluesy guitar string music playing from the rooftop bar above the store. Climbing the stairs, I'm surprised to see Devlin Frank leaning against the wall, his beautiful eyes locked on the singer with a soulful voice.

We don't know each other well. He's one of the best wide receivers in the league, and I'm a third-string running back and special teams kick returner entering his second professional year.

A nobody in Devlin's otherwise bright and shiny presence.

He locks eyes with me and nods his head, wordlessly inviting me over.

"Hey."

"You got out of there unscathed?" Devlin arches his brow.

I roll my eyes. "Not exactly."

"What happened?"

Taking the position next to him with my back against the wall, I mimic his posture by crossing my arms over my chest. "The dancer's boyfriend is Rick Stewart from the Nashville Notes. He met us in the parking lot. It was over before it started, but it should never have happened in the first place."

Devlin shakes his head, his eyes going back to the singer. "Jepson better watch his ass. Jaxson too."

And me, who is guilty by association, but Devlin's too nice of a guy to say that to my face.

"My, oh, my. A girl could have one hell of a night with you two." A woman in a bedazzled daisy duke outfit and bright cowboy boots saunters over to us, batting her fake lashes, a fruity drink in her hand. Not exactly sure where her accent is from, but she's definitely not from here.

Devlin chuckles and casts his eyes to the ground. "The two of us, huh?"

She nods and all but purrs, "I don't know if I could take both of you at the same time, but I'd be willing to try."

Going out with Jepson regularly, I've heard a plethora of creative and downright nasty things come out of women's mouths—things I didn't even know women thought about. Guys like Jepson and, I guess, guys like Devlin, attract women like this. When I'm by myself, nobody talks to me.

"That's very tempting, but I only have time for two more songs and then I have to get back to my room," Devlin says.

She looks him up and down and smiles. "I could come with you."

"I don't think my roommate would appreciate that."

She looks at me. "Are you not his roommate?"

Ha, I wish. "No, I'm not."

She juts her bottom lip and sighs. "Well, if you change your mind, I'll be at the bar."

"Does that happen to you often?" I ask as she walks away.

"Not lately." Devlin shakes his head nonchalantly. Just like on the football field, he's completely cool—always where Declan needs him to be, making each reception and every touchdown look effortless.

"Have you done that before?" The words are out before I can stop them.

"Done what?" He arches his brow.

"Uh…" I tilt my head toward the woman.

He chuckles. "What? Shared a woman with a teammate?"

I shrug, feeling stupid for asking. Honestly, I can't believe he's even talking to me right now. Yes, we're on the same team, but it shocked me that he and Rylie came out with us tonight. Or that Jepson had the balls to invite them. Devlin's two best friends are Declan Scott, star quarterback and heir to the Scott family fortune, which includes the Rocky Mountain Rangers football team, and Arnold "Aggie" Dunham, one of our star offensive linemen. Even though we are all working toward the same goal of being champions, they feel like the cool kids' club where I have never belonged. "Or anyone, I guess."

"Yeah, in high school and college. Mostly college. You?"

Blushing, I duck my head. "A few times in college before I dropped out."

"You dropped out of college?" Devlin claps his hands as the singer announces he's taking a break—showing how well he multitasks—and then he pushes off the wall and tilts his head toward the door.

I follow him out and down the stairs with my hands shoved in my pockets. "Yeah. I had to take care of my mom after they diagnosed her with cancer at the end of my sophomore year."

"Oh, wow. I'm sorry to hear that," Devlin wraps one

of his big hands on my shoulder and squeezes gently. "I'm almost afraid to ask..."

"She died four years ago," I answer the question no one ever wants to ask.

"Damn, man. Sorry."

We walk down Broadway toward the hotel in silence.

"Is that why you came on to the team mid-season last year?"

"Yeah. I've tried out for the Rangers three years in a row—since I missed my opportunity to be scouted in college—by attending their training camp. Last time, I scored well enough to impress the coaches, but unfortunately, Darnell Watkins was a little more impressive. They picked him up instead of me. When Doherty blew out his knee mid-season, Darnell moved up and I got the call," I shrug, realizing I'm rambling and need to shut up.

Devlin makes me nervous, and I know it's nothing he's doing on purpose. He's a good-looking man, probably one of the best in the league—if all the magazines and Instagram trolls are to be believed. Standing at six-foot-three, he's a little taller than most wide receivers. His eyes are this mesmerizing hazel which turns from blue to green to gray to almost yellow depending upon the light, and they pop against his darker skin. He has soft, kissable lips and the most dazzling smile I've ever seen. People use the term "lights up a room" when they talk about smiles, but his is the only one I've ever seen that truly does that. It also makes my stomach tie up in knots in a way I can't quite explain.

We walk through the hotel lobby and ride the

elevator up together. His room is to the left, while mine is to the right.

"Well, thanks for the talk." I shove my hands in my pockets and walk toward my room.

"We should hang out sometime, Rex," Devlin throws out casually. "Sleep tight and see you in the morning."

"I'd like that," I keep my tone blasé to match his, but on the inside, I feel like the cool kid just noticed me. "See you in the morning."

Chapter 1
Devlin

So, that was... weird.

Rex Williams, one of our kick returners and third-string running backs, has never talked to me. Honestly, I've never seen him talk to anyone other than Jepson and Jaxson Masters. Of course, I haven't gotten to know him either. Not because I'm a snob, but because I find him attractive and I'm not sure I could stop myself from flirting if presented the opportunity.

It's no secret I'm bisexual. I don't wear a rainbow flag on my jersey, nor do I talk about my love life to the press when they ask, but I've never denied it either. However, even though none of my teammates give me an attitude about it, the last thing I want is to make it weird with one of them.

The whole *you don't shit where you eat* mentality.

I have a couple of close friends in Declan and Aggie, but otherwise, catching footballs for the Rangers is a job I love, and that's it. I've always been a bit of a loner, and my aloofness makes me seem cooler to the casual observer than I really am, but it was weird he asked me about my sexual experiences.

Could Rex be interested?

No. That's fucking crazy talk. As far as I know, he's straight and spends most of his time with Jepson, who loves strip club dancers and starting fights. I don't know if Jepson is really a slut, but he carries himself like one.

Honestly, the whole Jepson-Jaxson-Rex dynamic is a complete mystery to me—even more so after hanging out with them for an hour tonight.

Besides, even if Rex was interested, what are either of us going to do about it? We couldn't openly date, not while on the same team. There are rules against dating cheerleaders and any other women connected to the team and I'm sure if the league thought it would come up, there'd be a no-fraternization policy between the players, too.

Right?

These are the thoughts dancing around in my head as I lay in bed praying for sleep. We play Nashville in the morning, and then we move on to the regular season. After last year's performance and our first two preseason games this year, we're projected to be one of the top teams this season. A lot is riding on us this year and all eyes will be on me and Declan as the dynamic duo. It's not just us—the entire team is gelling—but the press loves pitching us as the power couple.

Whatever.

Eye on the prize.

This season is about two things: a championship ring and a season of broken records.

Nothing else matters.

"That was embarrassing," I mutter to Declan as we take our seats on the plane heading home. We blew out Nashville forty-eight to seventeen, and they only got seventeen points playing against our third string. Everyone got a chance to play today.

Hell, I think even the water boy kicked a field goal.

Joking—but it makes my point.

"Yeah." Declan has a shit-eating grin on his face, which tells me he doesn't feel sorry for them one bit. "Wonder how the headlines will report the slaughter?"

"Whatever they say, it won't be satisfying to you. You didn't have to save the day—you fucking egomaniac."

"If I wasn't cocky, I'd barely have a personality." He flashes me a cheesy ass grin.

I roll my eyes and chuckle. He's one of my best friends, and he's actually a great guy who would give you the shirt off his back.

Of course, if he has a chance to pull it off in front of a group of hot women screaming for his attention, even better. The man loves to look at himself, especially when on the cover of a magazine.

Rex boards the plane with Jepson and Jaxson behind him. Damn, he is a good-looking guy—in a corn-fed kind of way. Reddish-blonde hair, brown eyes, about my height and weight and all muscle. Perfectly poised for corruption, which I'm sure Jepson Masters tries to introduce every chance he gets. "Hey, Rex. That was a nice touchdown today. Your first professional goal?"

"My first goal ever." Rex shrugs, as if to say it's no big deal. But it is a big deal, and I'm not going to let him downplay his accomplishment.

Luckily, Declan has my back as team captain. He glances up from his phone and acknowledges Rex with a chin tilt. "You did good. Eighty-seven-yard run, three missed tackles—you should be proud of yourself."

"Yeah, well, if the two of you hadn't put up twenty-four points before the end of the first quarter, I never would've played." Rex smiles at me. "So thank you."

Jepson smacks Rex on the arm. "Where are we sitting?"

Declan narrows his eyes. "Rick Steward changed positions and drew a personal foul penalty specifically so he could clobber you on the field today."

Jepson shrugs. "Yeah, I make friends easily."

"I guess we're lucky he didn't decide to take out his frustrations on your quarterback, huh?" Declan keeps his tone light, but the warning is there.

Jepson is smart enough to blanch, look away sheepishly, and mutter, "Yeah. I guess so."

I roll my eyes after he pushes past Rex, who suddenly looks uncomfortable in his skin.

"What happened to your eye, Jaxson?" Not that I don't already know.

Jaxson shakes his head and Rex sighs. "Well, thanks for the field time today."

"You'll get plenty more opportunities to show your stuff this season, I promise you." I hold up my fist, and Rex, his cheeks turning a gorgeous shade of pink, bumps it and then heads back a couple of rows to sit with his friends.

"The suicide squad," Declan mutters under his breath.

"I don't know. Rylie and I went out with them last night and honestly, I think the only troublemaker is Jepson. Jaxson's getting his ass handed to him by trying to protect his brother, and Rex doesn't know what to do. I don't think he has any other friends."

Declan chuckles. "You're not suggesting we adopt him, are you?"

"I'm just saying he doesn't seem like a bad guy."

Being on a team is weird. I mean, we're lumped together with a common goal, which weirdly makes us a family—so god help someone from another team who messes with one of our own. And yet, there are groups within the family and we bicker and faction like all large families do.

Much like Jepson, Jaxson and Rex are tight, Declan, Aggie and myself are thick as thieves. We'll be tight regardless of where our careers take us, even if we someday don another team's jersey. The tightly knit groups are usually formed by the positions we play— offense hangs with offense, defense with defense, and special teams with special teams. It's almost like high school cliques, which I always found bizarre considering we're grown-ass adults in our twenties and thirties.

Hell, some of us have wives and kids.

Speaking of which...

Aggie slumps into the seat across the aisle from us.

"What's up?" I furrow my brow.

He shakes his head. "My lawyer called. Ellen is contesting the divorce."

"Again?" My heart breaks for my best friend. He has been going through hell for months—no, scratch that, years—with this villainous woman and she will not let him go quietly. He's been living in my basement while she lives in his house and drives his car and lives her life off his bank account—of which she somehow got him locked out of. She's taken almost everything from him and still wants more.

"Yeah." He closes his eyes, letting me know he doesn't want to talk about it while surrounded by our teammates.

I reach across the aisle and pat his forearm. "Sorry, man."

Declan says nothing, meeting me in the eye and shaking his head. We all feel for the fluffy marshmallow because Aggie has to be the nicest man we know.

It's a three-hour plane ride home, and I pass the time decompressing by listening to music and filling out cross-word puzzles. Yep, I'm a big old geek, but only those close to me—like the two big guys sitting next to me and my older brother who also plays professional football—know the full extent. My brother Darren, who plays for Seattle

—our only real competition this season—fostered my love for strategy games when I was a kid. I frequent our local game shop to play DnD and other multiplayer games with a couple of groups when I'm in town. While most of my teammates get together on XBox and play PvP and other first-person shooter games, I'm logging onto WoW in my limited free time as a level 60 paladin, a level 55 Druid, or a level 65 shaman.

I've been playing since I was a kid, and although I don't have the time right now, I'm a pretty damn good DM. My basement is a testament to my geekdom, to include a custom-made gaming table and a collection of hand-painted miniatures.

Yes, I painted most of them.

As the plane touches down in Spring City and cell phones beep with incoming messages, Declan leans across me and smacks Aggie on the forearm. "You guys want to go out tonight?"

I raise my brow in Aggie's direction, but he shakes his head. "Nah. I'm going to lie low, just in case."

He's always worried he's going to run into Ellen somewhere out on the town and she's going to cause a major scene. I don't blame him one bit for being worried. The woman is crazy.

Declan sighs. "What about you?"

Locking eyes with Aggie, I shrug. "You want to chill out tonight and watch a movie, or do you need some time alone?"

Aggie shakes his head again. "You guys should go out and have a good time. I'll be fine at home."

I don't know why, but I can't stop myself from glancing a couple of rows back at the Rex. I wonder what he's doing tonight. Probably going to Diamonds and Pearls Cabaret, which I know for a fact is Jepson's stomping ground.

I smile at Declan. "What club are we going to?"

Spring City has an interesting vibe. Just under three-quarters of a million people large, it's a small town that grew quickly, but it'll never be as large as its big brother Denver. Most people don't realize that we have a bit of everything from evangelical churches to tech companies, military installations to professional sports teams. The ski slopes are two hours away, hot springs are one hour away, a decent size lake is forty-five minutes away, and one of the largest international airports in the country is ninety minutes away, and yet anyone who doesn't live here treats us like we're still the same small town we were fifty years ago. They'd never believe we have our very own underground kink club.

"We could go to the Pleasure House," Declan offers, as if he's reading my mind.

Personally, I'm not into kink—not that I know of—but the club is new, and I've been dying to check it out and Declan knows this.

Plus, we could never take Aggie there. The poor man would catch the vapors seeing some submissive tied up and flogged for an audience. He might Hulk-smash and try to rescue the damsel.

"The dungeon isn't open on Sundays, so we'd only be checking out the top floor, the main club access."

Damn. I shrug. "Probably for the best."

Declan chuckles because he knows me so well. "I bet we can get a private tour of the facilities if the owner is there."

"That'd be cool."

The plane rolls to a stop. We all grab our shit and wait to deplane. Declan slaps me on the shoulder as we make our way down the aisle. "I'll pick you up at nine."

"Sounds good."

Declan pulls into my driveway just before nine. "Where's Aggie?" He tilts his head to my missing limited edition Bronco, the one Aggie's been driving, considering Ellen somehow confiscated the keys to both of their cars.

"Ellen called, emailed, texted and WhatsApp'd to ask him to come over and pick up his suits and other clothes. It was too tempting an offer for him to ignore."

"Shit, we should probably go as backup."

"That's what I was thinking."

As Declan and I debate our plans, Aggie pulls into the garage looking like a drowned beaver. "Jesus Christ, what happened to you?"

He shakes his head. "She tried to seduce me and when I refused, she set all my clothes on fire in the driveway."

I suck in my breath. "You can't go over there anymore, man. That chick is unstable."

"Yeah, I know," Aggie sighs and looks at the Bronco. "Your car smells like smoke right now, but I'll detail it in the morning."

I slap my hand on top of his shoulder and squeeze. "It's okay."

Aggie looks from me to Declan and back to me. "I'm going to take a shower and go to bed."

As we watch Aggie—all formidable three hundred pounds of him—walk into my house as a completely defeated shell of a man, Declan and I make a silent decision. We follow our best friend into the house, kick off our shoes, and raid my fridge for snacks.

"What are you doing?" Aggie asks.

"We're chilling at home tonight, man. I'm thinking we will continue bingeing the Dawn of the Dead franchise, maybe gorge ourselves on pizza, and relax after a long day."

Declan nods his head. "Sounds good to me."

Aggie purses his lips as if he's going to argue, but then shakes his head slowly and slaps the wall. "You guys are good friends. Thanks."

I call the pizza place and put in our order while Declan makes the three of us a round of drinks. My thoughts drift back to Rex, and I wonder what the suicide squad—dammit, Declan, now I have that stuck in my head—is up to tonight.

I cannot start crushing on one of my teammates and yet, I have no one else filling my head.

Shit, this could get complicated quickly if I don't rein it in. At least Aggie has enough drama to keep me occupied for now.

Chapter 2
Rex

It's been a few weeks since that game in Nashville, and I haven't had one reason to talk to Devlin outside of a friendly head nod while we're passing each other on the practice field or in the locker room.

Things between Jepson and Jaxson have been weird lately—both of them are walking on eggshells, and I don't know why. Jaxson's been making himself scarce, and Jepson's been calling on me more to hang out. Although there are very few hours in the day when we are not training, it's still enough time to get in trouble and yet, Jepson seems to be avoiding it versus running head first, as usual.

The team is three and zero, and we played a fantastic game at home against Dallas. Emotions are high, and the energy is electric as we file into the locker room.

"We are partying tonight!" I say a little louder than I mean to. A series of hoots and hollers meets my statement, so maybe deep down I meant to say it loud enough that Devlin would hear. I catch his eye across the locker room for half a second before he nudges Aggie and says something I can't hear over the growing baritone cacophony of hyped-up and invigorated men.

"Strip club!" Jepson bellows.

"You got us kicked out of the last strip club, remember?" I elbow him playfully.

"That was in Nashville. We have a dozen other cities to be kicked out of this year. Besides, the ladies at Diamonds and Pearls love me." He flashes me that schoolboy grin he works so well and then smacks Jaxson on the shoulder. "What do you think? Want to head up to Denver tonight?"

"I don't know, Jeps. I'm not feeling it tonight, you know?" Jaxson says.

"Why? We just played a phenomenal game. Don't you want to celebrate?" Jepson argues.

I don't know what comes over me, but I feel the need to be the center of attention, specifically Devlin's attention, even if only for a minute. "Yeah! *Celebrate good times, come on,*" Wearing a towel, I sing Kool and the Gang's famous song while swinging my arms and ass before I hip-check Jaxson into his locker.

"Watch it, stupid ass," Jaxson shoves me back, his smile giving away his good humor. I glance over my shoulder, but Devlin isn't at his locker and that little display was for nothing.

I'm such a dork sometimes.

Greg McMillen, the offensive coordinator, makes his voice boom over the dull roar permeating the locker room. "No one leaves until the coach and the GM talk to you. Rex, do you hear me?"

"Yeah, Coach," I grumble, feeling completely stupid. His attention was not the one I desired. Dammit.

"I wonder what's going on?" Jepson says under his breath and nods in Aggie's direction, who is now sitting in front of his locker, pulling on his clothes like a condemned man with Devlin once again at his side.

Jaxson shakes his head. "Can't be good."

While we did well today, I didn't play much. Two kick returns totaling forty-three yards. Since I didn't work up a sweat and I'd rather shower at home, I change into my workout clothes while Jepson showers and we wait for management to show up. We don't have to wait long before Mike Monroe and Daniel Scott walk in, followed by Deacon and Declan Scott—the whole fam-damily minus their sister, Deidre, who most of us have never met in person.

My lowly third-string self certainly hasn't met her.

Declan, our star quarterback, takes residence center stage, halfway between his family and his team, with his arms crossed over his chest, his feet spread in a wide stance.

"Listen up," Deacon Scott's voice booms, shutting everyone up.

His father and our GM, Daniel, steps forward and speaks. "You played a great game today and I don't want to diminish this win, but it's early in the season and we still have a long way to go. Unfortunately, there are antics by members of this team overshadowing what should be our championship season. I see no reason to point out anyone specific as we are a team. We win as a team, and we lose as a team. One person's negative actions are the team's bad press."

Even though I do as little as possible to be noticed—I mean, I'm thankful to be playing professional ball at all and only hope I get opportunities to prove I belong here, so the last thing I want to do is cause negative light to shine on me—I feel like every person here wants to look in my direction. I mean, I know at least one or two of the jabs land in Jepson's basket.

The GM continues. "Club brawls, DUIs, personal dramas—these take away focus from what matters this season. Record-breaking stats and team cohesion. Since partying and reckless activities seem to be just as important to some of you as winning, I'm imposing a curfew on the team, as well as a gag order with the press, effective immediately. The only sanctioned interviews from members of this team will be coordinated by the President of Communications, Ms. Deidre Scott. Am I understood?"

A murmur of yeses filters through the assembled men.

Mike Monroe steps up. "Until I say otherwise, practice, travel and games will be from seven am to seven pm, Wednesday through Monday. Curfew is on your honor at eight pm. Fuck around and I find out, and we'll be discussing your future with the team. Next Wednesday, we will start in the briefing room, where I will discuss a couple of roster changes for the upcoming weeks. Your coaches are going to be pushing you hard to wring the absolute best out of each of you. If all goes well, you'll be too fucking tired for shenanigans."

I take a deep breath, trying not to feel scolded, even though I'm pretty sure I have nothing to feel guilty about.

Coach Monroe glances around the room. "Great game today. Be proud of yourselves, but be prepared for a few brutal weeks as we gear up for our toughest matchup this season against Seattle in week eight. Dismissed."

The locker room is silent until the coaches, the GM and both of the Scotts leave, and only then are there low rumbles of dissent amongst the players. Jepson slides his wallet and keys into his pocket, making eye contact with no one. He grumbles loud enough for only me and Jaxson to hear. "Pizza and Xbox tonight?"

I nod and follow the twins out of the locker room as quickly as possible. Right before I leave, I glance over my shoulder in Devlin's direction to find his eyes on me.

Is that a look of curiosity or condemnation?

Am I guilty by association in Devlin's mind?

I know Jepson and Jaxson are great guys. Yeah, they've got some childhood traumas to work through—things they don't talk about to anyone including me—but otherwise, they are good guys with quirks that might make them unattractive to an outside observer. Jepson comes off like an arrogant asshole—which equally repels as well as attracts the ladies—while Jaxson is a scarred and tattooed introverted recluse.

I guess I'm the third wheel.

The bland vanilla center in an otherwise weird and wild cookie sandwich.

Maybe I should get myself a hobby—one away from the team for my off time. I used to love role-playing games and although it's been years since I've logged onto a server, I'm still a member of an online guild. Instead of playing first-person shooter games with Jepson on Xbox all night, like I have since joining the Rangers, maybe I should go to one of the local game shops and see what's new in the fantasy realm of orcs, druids, and blood elves.

Maybe I should take in my guitar and get it restrung?

Maybe I should think about dating again?

No. No more online dating bullshit. The truth is, I'm not really into it. I've met a handful of women and gone on a couple of dates with each, but nothing ever clicks for me.

Not sure if it's a woman I'm looking for, either.

Honestly, I don't know what I want or what's wrong with me. I can look at a person and understand what's conventionally attractive about them. Hair, eyes, shape, smile, personality, sense of humor, fashion sense... the list goes on, but I rarely find myself attracted to a person I haven't formed a bond with. In high school, I was the only kid who wasn't completely focused on getting laid. Most of the time it didn't occur to me, and during my senior year, a few of the guys on the team asked me why. *Why don't you have a girlfriend or a boyfriend?* They didn't care if I was gay; they just wanted to know why I wasn't obsessed about getting my dick sucked like they were.

Then I went to college where it was more of the same. My roommate, Tim, was a very sexual guy who was into trying everything three times. His motto was simple: Try it once to see if you like it. Twice, to make sure the first time wasn't a fluke. And a third time, to be extra sure.

Tim was the life of the party, whether there was a party going on or not. He was openly bisexual and so unbelievably comfortable with who he was that he attracted all kinds of people to dance within his sphere of influence. Although he was a little wild for me, he was a great roommate who invited me to tag along wherever he went. My freshman year I could lie low between football and school, going to the occasional party so I didn't seem like a complete outcast, but my sophomore year, Tim met someone who matched his energy perfectly, and she was super focused on playing with me.

Dalia was Tim in female form. Wild and up for anything, my virginity was her catnip and her number one obsession. I liked her and Tim well enough, and I knew they were attractive by societal standards. After hearing them go at it a couple of times in the room we shared, I gave in and experimented with both of them.

What's weird is that even though I don't crave sex, when I'm having it, I have a great time. I enjoy every touch and taste, but I particularly like the sounds. I don't know what it is about the moans, gasps, and guttural groans that get me going, but they do.

I can go to the strip club with Jepson to watch the dancers and enjoy their aesthetic beauty, but it doesn't turn me on. Watch porn on mute, nothing, but hear the symphony that is sex—instant hard-on.

Like I said, I know I'm different from most guys and on the asexual spectrum. That doesn't bother me. The question is, how will I have a fulfilling relationship if I don't think about initiating sex? How can I admit my sexual idiosyncrasies to a new partner without driving them away? I don't want to fake it in the beginning, only to have it come out later—as I know it will.

Perhaps I'm destined to be the third wheel for the rest of my life?

Our last Monday off for god knows how long and I'm checking out the third gaming store within a ten-mile radius of my house. It's amazing how fast the games change and yet basically stay the same. Expansion packs with new characters, new levels, and new quests—I'm going to have to learn new keystrokes before I can level up my characters.

After talking to a couple of guys at the first two stores, I'm checking out this shop more for the fun of it. They have comics, games, and a coffee bar that sells sandwiches and baked goods. In the back, there are private gaming rooms where people hold weekend-long tournaments. The books, posters, card packs, dice, and overarching vibe of the shop fill me with nostalgia. Yes, I was a jock in high school, but I was also a WoW-playing geek—not that I thought me or my online friends were geeks. It's just what they called us and we embraced the title without qualms.

Life was simpler back then.

"Rex?" Someone says my name, causing me to spin around with the fanfic book in my hands.

Smiling at me from across the room is one of the best-looking men I've ever met. I wonder if my feelings for Devlin are fan-based or true attraction. He's perfect in so many ways. Beautiful, kind, talented, smart...and a game-playing geek?

"What are you doing here?" I fumble with the book in my hand before setting it back on the rack.

His smile morphs into a knowing smirk. "I play with a Monday group when I can in the back. Are you a gamer?"

"I, uh..." I glance down and back up again. He makes me nervous, which I both love and hate. "I was when I was a kid. It's been a few years, but I was thinking about getting back into it. What got you into gaming?"

"My older brother when I was in elementary school."

"Ah." I fidget, unsure what to do with my hands. "So, are you playing a game right now?"

"We just wrapped up. I was on my way to grab a sandwich. Have you had lunch yet?" Devlin flashes that thousand-watt smile, and I swear my knees get weak.

"Not yet."

"Want to?"

"Sure," my voice squeaks, and I quickly hide it by coughing into my hand. "What did you have in mind?"

"There's a great NY-style deli a few blocks from here. The owner makes a fantastic cheesesteak." He uses his fingers and offers a chef's kiss to the universe.

"Great. I'll follow you," I offer.

"Let me grab my stuff and I'll drive. You can leave your car here," Devlin chucks me on the arm and then dashes out of sight into the back room. Butterflies, the likes of which I've never felt before, rumble in my tummy. I'm going to lunch with Devlin Frank. I've been fantasizing about this moment—spending time with him, finding some common ground with which to build a friendship, or more—for almost a year.

He jogs out from the back with a backpack slung over his shoulder. "You ready?"

"Yeah." I follow him outside to a dark green, almost black convertible Mini Cooper. Chuckling, I shake my head. "When and where did you get this?"

He laughs. "I'm test-driving it for a week. It's like their top-of-the-line everything, and the dealership wants to give it to me if I'm willing to do a few promotional pictures in it."

"Aren't we too tall for it?"

"Nah. It's roomier than it looks." He hops into the driver's seat and gives the passenger's seat a challenging pat. "Come on, Rex. Don't be scared."

I slide in and he's right—my six-foot-two frame melts into the seat like butter. I'm not one for convertibles, so I'm curious about what a hard top would feel like. "This isn't so bad."

"Nah." Devlin skirts in and out of traffic, driving

more than the two blocks to show off the agility of the smaller ride. "If you like it, I could probably get you a deal with the dealership. The owner is champing at the bit to get the Rangers endorsement."

"Can we do that?" I have to admit, it's a smooth ride. Pretty sure Jepson would clown me if I suggested checking one out, though.

"Maybe not on behalf of the Rangers, but as a professional footballer, sure." He zips into a small parking lot and finds rockstar parking in front of the deli. "Hope you're hungry. Gideon loves me, so we'll be well-fed."

It's a little after one on a workday, so most of the lunch crowd is gone, and the deli is relatively empty. We grab a booth in the corner as a tall guy with dark hair approaches us with a big smile. "Devlin. How are you doing?"

"Doing good, Gideon. How's the wife and cats?"

"Claws of Fury is doing good." He laughs and looks at me. "That's the cat, not the wife."

"Oh," I chuckle.

"What can I get you guys?" Gideon asks.

I motion to Devlin. "I trust your judgment."

"Two ten-inch cheesesteaks—put the works on mine. Do you like mushrooms, onions, and bell peppers?" Devlin asks me.

"Yeah."

"Okay, put the works on both of them. Basket of fried things, and I'll take an iced tea." He raises his brow at me.

"Iced tea works for me as well."

"Sweet or regular?" Gideon asks.

"Half and half?" I prompt and Devlin nods to say, "Same."

As Gideon walks away, Devlin leans back in his chair and throws an arm up over the top of the padded back-rest. "So, Rex, which games do you play?"

"Uh, in high school, I played World of WarCraft mostly and dabbled in Final Fantasy, Fortnite, and Minecraft. I thought with the lockdown, maybe getting online and lying low was best for my future. I'm not an amazing player like you, so even the smallest infraction could get me kicked off the team. You know?"

Gideon walks up with a plate of fried everything—mushrooms, zucchini, onion rings, pickles and fries—as well as two iced teas. "Be right back with your sandwiches."

"Thanks." Devlin grabs napkins out of the dispenser and hands me a couple. "You may not get a lot of opportunity to show off your skills on game day, but I think you've impressed a few people during practice. Who knows? Keep kicking ass and showing up our second-string running back and they might move you up."

I pop a fry in my mouth. "I'm just thankful to be here."

"You got to want more than that, Rex. The coaches want to know you are hungry for that next level. Show them in practice and when the opportunity comes, they'll know you are ready." Devlin nods at Gideon as he sets our sandwiches down. The aroma makes my mouth water and my stomach growl. "Thanks."

"Damn, these look good," I say, slightly embarrassed by his mild scolding, or should I think of it as mentoring?

"They are." Devlin takes a big bite, digging into his food with enthusiasm. I follow suit and for a few minutes, we eat in silence.

"What game were you playing today?" I ask, hoping to veer us away from football for the moment.

"Pathfinder. That group has been playing together since they were kids. They let me jump in when I'm around, knowing my schedule is unpredictable." He shrugs. "It's fun, although I'd love to get a game going at my house."

"That'd be cool. I never got into tabletop games—I didn't have anyone to play with—even though I've always been curious."

Devlin stares at me for a moment, as if he's trying to figure out a mystery. "Well, if I get a game going, I'll invite you over."

"Does Aggie play?"

"He doesn't, although I'm sure he would try if I asked him to."

"He's your roommate, right?" I ask, divulging that I know more about him than he might think.

"He is, for the moment. I'm sure you've heard a rumor or two about his wife."

I shrug. "Not much, but what I've heard sounds horrible."

"Yeah," Devlin looks away. "Aggie's a good guy and deserves better. He's one of my best friends and has been living with me while waiting for his divorce to finalize."

"You're a good friend. He's lucky to have you," I say with a hint of jealousy, which is baffling. I don't begrudge Aggie any kindness he has in his life, especially considering the shit he's gone through, but I wish I could get as close to Devlin.

Is it friendship I desire, or more?

Chapter 3
Devlin

How crazy was it to run in Rex today—at a game shop, of all places? Looks like we have more in common than I originally thought.

"Tell me about yourself, Rex?"

He looks up at me in surprise, popping the last of his sandwich into his mouth. "What do you want to know?"

Shrugging, I toss a fried pickle into my mouth. "I don't know. I know you lost your mom a few years ago, but what about your dad? Do you have siblings? A girlfriend? What made you want to play for the Rangers?"

Rex wads up his napkin and throws it on his empty plate. I love a man that can eat, as I also love food.

"My dad skipped out on us when I was a kid, so I'm not sure where he is today. Actually, that's not true. I'm pretty sure I know where he is, but I have no intentions of finding him."

That one statement has an ominous tone to it, and I feel like it's best to leave it alone for the moment.

He continues. "No brothers or sisters. Not a lot of family to speak of, honestly. I'm from a small town in Nebraska, so there wasn't much there, and besides the Denver Mustangs, the Rangers are the closest thing to a home team. Plus, I've been watching you guys build your offensive lineup over the last few years and deep down, I want to be a part of that."

I reach across the table and pat his hand. "You are."

He blushes and I find it damn near irresistible, but I can't help notice that he skipped the girlfriend question.

"What about you? I know your brother plays for Seattle and your dad was a wide receiver, too. Right?"

Rex leans back and grabs a clean napkin, shredding it into tiny pieces. I noticed he did that at the strip club in Nashville a few weeks ago, too.

"Yep. Eight seasons with Baltimore, four seasons with Atlanta, where he retired." My father was also a wide receiver, mostly second-string, although he had several starts throughout his career and a few shortly held record-breaking stats.

"How does he feel about you blowing away all his records?" Rex asks tentatively.

I flash him a big smile. "My father loves it when Darren or I break any record, even his. He wants us to succeed. There's no ego there."

"Wow. He sounds amazing."

"Yeah, he is."

Gideon walks up at that moment with two to-go containers. "For your sweet tooth later."

"Thanks," I chuckle, already knowing what's inside—

three different cannolis. Rex's eyes go wide and his mouth forms a perfect O when he takes a peek.

"Do you think you'll be logging on tonight?" I ask.

"I'm going to try. I'll have to download the expansion packs, and I haven't checked on my characters in years. So, I might be starting from scratch."

"Give me your number and I'll text you my handles." I hold my cell in my hand, feeling smooth that I'm getting his number without straight up asking for it. "Once you get yourself online, you can message me and we'll meet up in the fantasy realm. Worst case, I can help you level up your new characters quickly."

Rex rattles off his number, and I immediately send him a text.

"Well, I guess I better get home and see if my computer can handle the new expansion packs." Rex stands up and stretches his arms over his head. The bottom of his T-shirt rides up enough to flash me a peek at his toned abs and a hint of red hair forming a treasure trail.

Diverting my eyes, I climb out of the bench seat. "I know a guy who can help you with that."

"With what?" Rex reaches over and grabs both of our to-go containers, his wallet in his hand.

"I got it, man," my wallet also in my hand.

"I can't let you pay for lunch," he argues.

I arch my brow. "I invited you, remember? You'll get me another time."

"Are you sure?"

"Yeah. I like buying the first time. That way you'll

feel compelled to do this again." I flash him a flirty smile, unable to stop myself.

Again, a light blush hits his cheeks and I love it. "I'd like that."

After paying the check, Gideon offers me and Rex a hearty handshake and well wishes for a successful season, and then we're driving back to the game shop.

"I might need to test drive a hard top someday," Rex says casually, sliding his hand over the supple leather.

"Can I give my guy your number? He'll call and schedule a test drive." I grin when he looks my way with raised brows.

"You have a guy for everything, don't you? What was the other guy you mentioned earlier?"

"That's my computer guy. He hand-built both my tower and my laptop. He can look at your setup, tweak it with whatever parts are needed, or build you something from scratch."

"I might need that. My gaming PC is six years old."

For some reason, I want to prolong our afternoon together. This isn't a date, even though I'd like it to be and I want more time with him. "Well, if you want, I can ask my guy to come tonight. I'll bring him over myself."

"You want to come to my place?" Rex stares at me, and I can't tell what he's thinking. Am I overstepping and making him uncomfortable?

I shrug. "I mean, I don't have to."

"No, I'd like you to come over." He bites his lip and chews on his cheek. "I need an hour or two to clean, though."

Chuckling, I pull into the parking spot next to his red truck. "I can give you that. Let me call Chris and see if he's available. How's six o'clock sound to you?"

"Sounds like we're having dinner."

Chris couldn't make it, but he sold me a robust laptop similar to the one I upgraded to months ago. I'm going to gift it to Rex, whether or not he wants me to. The simple fact is, even if he is straight and we can be nothing more than friends—which is where my brain should be even though it keeps drifting into relationship territory—he's a nice guy and would benefit from forming more friendships on the team.

It would be good for his reputation to put some distance between him and Jepson, that's for sure.

Plus, I don't have any other players to game with.

The two-car garage on his house is open. He texted and told me to roll right in, which I do. I grab all the computing gear—both his and mine—and look up in time to find Rex opening the door to his house. He's a vision in joggers and a tight T-shirt stretched over his broad chest with a black apron tied around his trim waist.

"Are you cooking?" I ask at the same time a rich, buttery aroma wafts out of the kitchen.

"Yeah." He runs his fingers through his thick reddish-blond hair. "I like to tinker and rarely have an excuse to do so. Hopefully, you like it."

"I'm sure I'll love it."

"Do you need help?" He tilts his chin to the pile in my arms.

"Nope." Walking into his house, I'm instantly intrigued by the understated decor and mid-demolition/remodel state of a few walls. He lives well below his means—the lowest-paid running back still makes more than half a million a year—which is most likely a testament to his near-poverty upbringing. I could tell by the little he's told me about his mom and hometown, he didn't grow up with much.

On the other hand, I'm second generation professional football and one of the highest-paid wide receivers in the league at just over twenty-eight million a year, and that doesn't include sponsorships or endorsement deals. Still, I like his style. His place feels less clinical than mine —comfortable and lived in.

As if he's reading my mind, he clears his throat and motions to the living room. "It's a work in progress."

"I like it." I set the equipment down on one of two leather recliners facing two giant flat screens. "It seems like you're already set up for gaming."

"Jepson and Jaxson have a similar setup at their place. We play Call of Duty and GTA a lot over XBox."

"Well, now you have options with me." Unable to stop myself, I wink as I hand him the cardboard box. "This is for you. As I told you earlier, Chris has a parent-teacher conference tonight, so I had him build you a gaming laptop. It's almost identical to mine, and he already pre-installed WoW. All you have to do is login and configure your account."

"How much do I owe him?" Rex sets the box down and opens it, running his big hand almost lovingly over the matte black and neon green case.

"It's on me." I pull my laptop out of my bag, the two pieces of equipment are nearly identical except mine is matte black and electric blue. Rex says nothing, which causes me to bring my eyes up.

"I can't let you do that." He shakes his head again.

"Why not? Consider it a welcome-to-the-team gift. Besides, I've been dying to have someone on the team to raid with." I pull cables out of my bag, not taking no for an answer. "Do you have to man whatever's cooking, or can you set up your gear and configure your account?"

"It has to bake for another fifteen minutes."

"Enough time to power up, log in, and let the servers do their thing."

Rex sits down on the loveseat between the two recliners and I take a seat next to him. He gives me his Wi-Fi password and then we're sitting in comfortable silence while he logs in and configures his account and I run HDMI cables to the big TV screens.

"Man, this computer is fast," Rex mumbles reverently under his breath.

"Yeah, Chris is a gamer and knows how to build good equipment."

"I'm glad he didn't get a look at my old tower. He would've laughed his ass right out of here."

"Awww, I wouldn't have let him do that to you." I elbow him at the same time a timer rings in the kitchen.

Rex sets his laptop down and stands. "Are you hungry?"

"I'm always hungry." I also put my laptop down on the table and stand.

He stares at me for a second, a coy smile on his lips. "This way."

Pointing to a table with two place settings, he tells me to take a seat. There's another wall missing sections in his makeshift dining room and plastic drop cloths taped haphazardly over the openings, which leads me to believe he's expanding the kitchen. "Do you have a background in construction?"

He comes back with two plates and frowns. "No."

"Are you doing this yourself?" I wave my hand over the room before letting my eyes come down to my plate. "Holy crap, this looks fancy."

"It's like poor man's beef Wellington, but I used filet mignon."

"Doesn't sound poor at all." My mouth waters at the smell rising from the buttery, flaky crust.

Rex shrugs. "Would you like red wine, or maybe a porter?"

"You know, I think I'll stick with water. I want nothing to overpower this amazing meal."

"Good idea." Rex sits beside me and lifts his fork, opting to do the same.

We eat for a few minutes in silence while I actively remind myself not to moan out loud. Damn, this is good and way better than anything I can cook. I'm a charcuterie board kind of guy, buying and laying out all the good stuff the deli manager throws in my cart. Outside of that, I'm a whiz on the Grubhub app. Considering I only saw Rex four hours ago, I'm super impressed with what he did in the limited time.

After taking a couple of bites and realizing I'm devouring versus savoring each morsel, I wipe my mouth before clearing my throat. "You were saying about the remodel."

Rex looks up from his plate. "I haven't found a contractor yet, so I started without them. Probably a bad idea. YouTube will only take you so far."

Glancing around, I wonder what other rooms are mid-construction. "May I ask you a potentially sensitive question?"

He nods. "Sure."

"Why did you buy a fixer-upper versus a new build on the north end where most of us live? You could have designed the exact house you wanted in my neighborhood." As soon as the words come out of my mouth, I remember what he said about his upbringing. "Sorry, that's probably a stupid question."

He shakes it off. "It's cool. I told you my dad took off when I was a kid. I was maybe four or five. Pretty sure he's in prison right now, if not dead. He was—" Rex sighs "—well, if someone can be addicted to something, I'm sure he was. Drugs, alcohol, gambling, sex—I think he tried in the beginning with my mom, but eventually his demons won. He left us with less than nothing, draining the bank account and leaving my mom with tens of thousands of dollars in credit card debt. She worked at a factory until the day she could no longer physically stand, but their benefits were practically non-existent, so when she got sick—I mean, by the time she was diagnosed—it was too late. We'd rented the same one-bedroom shit-hole apartment my entire life and my bed was behind the couch. My mom was never home because she worked two jobs and once I was old enough, I was also working when I wasn't in sports."

He stands up and walks into the living room, returning seconds later with a framed photograph. Handing it to me, he retakes his seat. Staring back at me is a woman in her mid-twenties with long, beautiful red hair and freckles. She's got a radiant smile as she sits and stares at the camera with her arms wrapped around a jubilant six- or seven-year-old boy. "She's beautiful."

"Yeah, she was. It was her dream to see me play professional ball. Even though we couldn't afford it, she pushed me to play every school sport available, hoping for a scholarship. Football, wrestling, baseball. Although we had nothing, she always got me the gear I needed." He takes the picture back from me and stares at it for a moment, a sweet smile spreading on his lips. This vulnerable moment he's willing to share with me makes me want to wrap my arms around him and never let go.

Rex glances around his place. "Back to the remodeling question. When the Rangers called and moved me out here, I wanted a place I could buy with cash. The organization gave me a significant signing bonus for showing up within hours, and I used that to buy this place. I figure, no matter what happens with my professional career, at least I'll have a home that no one can take away from me. Owning a three-bedroom home with a yard is all my mom ever dreamed about. That and watching me play professional ball."

I wrap my fingers around his forearm and squeeze. "I'm sure she is super proud of you right now."

"Yeah," He looks down at my hand and then away, his eyes darting around the space. "If you know of any general contractors, send them my way. With our schedule, I'll never get this place remodeled on my own."

"I bet the Scotts know a few. The non-football side of the family is in real estate, so I'm sure they know all the local contractors. Want me to ask?" I squeeze his forearm again and then let go to push back from the table and clear our plates.

"That would be good." He grabs our glasses and leads me into the kitchen. "Just set the plates down there. I'll clean up later."

"No way, man. My mama would skin me if she knew someone cooked me an amazing meal like this and then I didn't do the dishes."

He chuckles. "Fine. We'll do them together."

Fifteen minutes later, our leftovers are wrapped up and the dishes are in the dishwasher. Rex offers me a beer, which I take, and we both grab a recliner, our computers in our laps. For the next two hours we quest, giving Rex time to orientate himself with the keystrokes and shortcuts. I take him on a couple of lower-level raids I can run by myself, building up his XP and gold in the process.

"This is the best date I've ever been on," he chuckles.

A spark of hope ignites in my chest, but I tamp it down. "What do you mean?"

He motions to the screen where his character stands still and I run around killing all the NPCs. "I just stand here and look pretty while you do all the work to gift me gold and armor and weapons."

"Interesting way to look at it, but if you want to call it a date, I'm okay with it."

Chapter 4
Rex

Glancing out of the corner of my eye, I watch Devlin as he sits in my guest recliner, running his character through the dungeon. Never in my life did I think he'd be hanging at my house, playing a game on my big screen TVs—with me. When he suggested coming over, I got nervous because I know my home isn't anywhere near his standard of living.

Still, it's been a nice evening—one I will never forget.

I wish I knew how to flirt. I'd give anything to subtly let him know I not only like him but LIKE him. Sure, we've only spent a few hours together, but I already know I think of him differently than I do Jepson or Jaxson. Is that what attraction is? Noticing all the nuances about the object of your desire that it takes days, weeks, or months to notice on someone else?

If I had the talent, I would draw Devlin's beautiful eyes in intricate detail from memory alone, but the only thing I can tell you about Jepson and Jaxson's eyes is that they are blue. The left side of Devlin's smile tilts up a little more than the right side, and when he flashes that million-dollar smile, a small dimple appears on his cheek.

"What do you think?" Devlin's silky voice pulls me out of my fantasies.

I quickly glance up at the paused game. "About what?"

He chuckles. "Is this a good place to stop for the night?"

"Sure."

Logging off, he closes his laptop and sets it on the side table before lowering the footrest of the recliner. "I've already broken curfew. I should probably get my ass home."

"Oh crap." I check my watch to find it's already fifteen after eight. "I totally spaced curfew."

Devlin stands and stretches his arms over his head, his muscular thighs flexing in his workout shorts. His body, like his face, is pure perfection—every muscle intricately defined like a bronzed work of art. "No worries. Tonight was worth the risk."

I don't know how to respond to that. "How would they know?"

"I suppose they wouldn't unless something happened after hours like a traffic ticket or car accident, bar brawl, DUI, etc."

"Aggie won't tell on you?" I tease.

"Nah. He'd never betray me." Devlin unhooks the HDMI cable from the TV, wraps it up and places it and his laptop in the bag. I walk him to the door, hitting the button to open the garage while he places his bag in the passenger seat.

All of a sudden, I'm overcome with a wave of awkwardness and a deep desire to kiss him goodnight while holding open the driver's door to his car.

"When can we do this again?" I ask with my heart in my throat.

Devlin smiles, his eyes moving down to my lips before he chuckles and imperceptively shakes his head, as if he's dismissing a thought. "Which part? Playing games or hanging out?"

"Both."

"I usually get online for an hour before I go to bed every night. It helps me relax. As far as hanging out, I'll come over anytime you invite me—especially if you're going to cook."

I press my lips together and nod. "I'd like that."

"I'll see about getting you a couple of contractor names and numbers tomorrow. Were you serious about test-driving one of these?" He pats the top of the headrest of his Mini Cooper.

I shrug. "Sure. Why not."

"I'll send Bill a text. I'm sure he'll call you first thing tomorrow," Devlin smiles again, his eyes hitting the ground. "Thanks for dinner, Rex."

"It was my pleasure. Thanks for the computer," I run my hand through my hair and take a step back, trying to break this gravitational pull he has on me. "Are you sure I can't pay for it?"

"Absolutely." He winks while shoving his hands in his pockets.

Seconds tick by as a stifling silence descends between us. This is the moment I think normal people on a date lean in for a kiss, but this isn't a date. Right?

"You know, that stuff I told you about my dad—" I look away, slightly ashamed "—I've never talked about that to anyone before."

"Not even Jepson and Jaxson?" He arches his brow.

Shaking my head, I meet his eye. "Not the whole story. For some reason, we stay on the fringe of deep childhood trauma talks when we hang out."

"Why'd you tell me?"

I shake my head. "I don't know, but it felt right."

"Your secret is safe with me." He worries his lip, as if he's thinking through his next words. "I wanted to hug you while you were talking about your mom, but I was afraid I'd freak you out."

I contemplate my potential reaction had he done that. As players, we see each other physically vulnerable every day. Whether we are naked in the locker rooms or injured on the field, we rarely share emotions other than frustration or celebration directly related to the game. There are back slaps, butt slaps, helmet slaps and celebratory hugs, but most of us keep the personal stuff buried deep from each other. "I think I would've liked that."

"The offer still stands." He pulls his hands out of his pockets and spreads his arms wide. "Anytime you want a hug, let me know."

Now I feel ridiculous and shake my head, chuckling under my breath. "Get out of here."

Devlin also chuckles and then reaches out and chucks me on the shoulder with his fist. "Talk to you later."

I watch him pull out of my driveway and drive out of sight before I close the garage door and lock up for the night. If you had told me when I woke up this morning that I would spend the evening hanging out with my number one crush, I would have checked your temperature expecting a high-grade fever accompanied by hallucinations.

Wow—Devlin wanted to hug me. My mom was affectionate, but outside of her cure-all hugs, I didn't grow up with a lot of physical touch. I'm not sure I would have been able to stop myself from melting into his embrace had he wrapped his arms around me.

It's been a long time since I felt that kind of comfort.

I grab my phone and notice a slew of missed texts from Jepson.

5:30pm: Want to grab dinner?

5:45pm: Yo! Where are you at?

6:15pm: I'm going to grab a burger. I've got to get out of the house for a bit. If you get this, meet me at Burger Barn downtown.

> 7:30pm: Guess you're busy. I hope you're on an epic date or some shit. Want to grab breakfast tomorrow? We need to get out before the lockdown becomes official. Ya know?

I text him back.

> 8:20pm: Sorry I missed you. I think I'm going to test drive a Mini Cooper tomorrow. Want to do breakfast and then go to the dealership with me?

> You and a tiny car? Fuck yeah, I want to come.

> Haha. Yuck it up, buddy. See you in the morning.

I meet Jepson and Jaxson near the AutoMall for breakfast. After we order our meals, I lean back in my chair, my gaze bouncing between the two of them. Something is up, but I have no idea what it could be. Jepson is being super nice to Jaxson, who is quieter than normal.

These two make me crazy sometimes. I wonder what life would be like if I had a twin or even a brother. Do Devlin and his brother have weird interactions and a lifetime of secrets like these two?

"Were you on a date last night?" Jepson asks after sucking down half of his orange juice.

I shake my head. "I haven't had a date in weeks."

"No interesting prospects? That sucks. What did you do last night?"

Shit. I don't want to tell them I'm spending time with Devlin because I'm afraid my feelings for the hunky wide receiver will be all over my face. "I got a new computer yesterday and spent last night gaming."

"Which game?" Jaxson brings his head up from his phone. I normally play with them over XBox and that's it.

"WarCraft."

"We didn't know you played that." Jaxson glances at Jepson, who shakes his head.

I shrug. "You don't play it, so I had no reason to tell you."

"Is it any fun?" Jepson asks.

Nodding, I spread my napkin across my lap as the server arrives with our food. "I used to play when I was a kid, so there's some nostalgia there. What did you guys do last night?"

Jepson and Jaxson exchange a look.

"Well, as you know, I went out for a burger," Jepson says plainly.

"I, uh, went for a drive," Jaxson says without looking at me.

Damn, these guys are weird sometimes. They hold things close until whatever drama blows over, then they tell me about it nonchalantly, like it was never a big deal. Considering this time I'm also holding something close, I let it go.

Who am I kidding? I always let it go. "Okay."

We eat our meals and switch our conversation topic to the team and the new lockdown. Instead of bitching as I expect, Jepson assumes some of the responsibility and then does something that shocks me. He apologizes to both Jaxson and me about any bad press he's brought our way and promises to do better, leaving both his brother and me speechless.

The rest of the morning proceeds as expected, with Jepson playing carnival music from his phone when I climb into the Mini Cooper—the brothers bonding as they laugh. Deep down, I knew he was going to do it. I mean, how could he not, considering it was the first thing I thought yesterday when Devlin walked up to his car?

Devlin. I wonder what he's doing today? The temptation to text him this morning was strong, but I tamped it down because the last thing I want to do is come across like an eager puppy. Still, you know damn well I'll be logged on tonight, waiting for him to show up.

The Mini Cooper, while a fun little ride, is an expense I don't want to take on right now. I'm thinking of ways to let the sales agent down easily when Jepson takes the attention off of me by asking about a lease trade-in sitting on the lot. Two hours later, I'm leaving in my old red Dodge pickup and Jepson is driving away in a hot Jaguar F-Type sports car. He has plans tonight that he doesn't elaborate on, and I don't ask, but considering how excited he is, I'm assuming it's a date.

As I'm driving home, my phone beeps with a voice message from Devlin.

"Hey, man. I hope your day is going well. I got you a

contractor. Mel Martinez with Woman's Work Remodels —an all-female crew. They recently did all the finish work with the Springs City Fire Department on a city program to build four temporary homes for fire victims and finished a portion of the presentation center at SCCU. Carpentry, plumbing, electrical, landscaping— they do it all and come highly recommended. I'll send you their contact card."

Clicking on the number, I'm greeted by a woman's voice, the sound of saws running in the background. "This is Mel."

"Hi. My name is Rex, and I'm calling about a potential remodel?"

"Oh yeah? What are you looking to have done?" The machinery sounds quiet down as I presume she walks away from them.

"Well, I have a house in the old Pinehurst neighborhood that could use some love."

"Pinehurst? My electrician lives in that area. Great bones with lots of potential. We could come by tonight if you like."

"Wow. Okay. Tonight would be good," If the coach's words hold, Tuesdays will be the only day to conduct business for the foreseeable future.

"Does six work for you?"

"Yeah." I rattle off my address.

"Great. Can I also have your last name, Rex?"

"Williams."

"And can I ask how you got my name and number?"

"Uh, well, from my teammate. I play for the Rangers and I guess the Scotts know all the right people to call."

"You're a football player?" She sounds skeptical.

I'm not used to being recognized as a player, so any association with the team feels insincere—like I'm bragging or something. I guess in some ways I still can't believe I finally made it. "Yeah, I am."

"That's cool. Sorry for all the questions, but as a female crew, we like to know whose house we're walking into beforehand. Anyone the Graysons or Scotts recommend is cool with us. We'll see you tonight, Rex."

"Okay. Bye." Hanging up the phone, I send a text to Devlin.

> They are coming tonight at six. Wow! After months of living in a mess, I might have a complete house soon. Thanks.

> That's great. I can't wait to see your remodeled home.

> Will you be online tonight?

> I will be. Look for me around nine.

> Sounds good.

And just like that, I have a virtual date with Devlin tonight.

Chapter 5
Devlin

Nearly every night over the last five weeks, I've met Rex online for an hour or two so we can quest and chat. We both have headsets that allow us to talk in real-time while running our characters through campaigns, but I have found a sense of possessiveness grips my heart when we join raids with other players who try openly flirting with him.

Five weeks and I have no idea where I stand with my teammate who, despite my attempt to the contrary, I find myself more and more attracted to. Sometimes I think he's flirting with me, but when I flirt back, he seems oblivious to my feelings.

Is he not interested?

Hell, I'm still not sure if he's straight or not.

We've also been on lockdown for five weeks, and the team is getting restless. On the field, we've been fantastic despite a loss in week six that never should have happened. We play Seattle next Sunday, and I've arranged dinner with my brother after the game and a late-night flight the next day home. Part of me wants to invite Rex, but considering our relationship seems to be a secret—we barely acknowledge each other on the field or in the locker room and I'm not exactly sure why—I don't know if that is a good idea.

I think I intimidate Rex on the field, which I guess I understand. After our dinner, I had a down-low conversation with Greg, our offensive coordinator, and Darius, the special teams coordinator, about pushing Rex to see what he can do. Although I have no say in the matter, I'm less than impressed with our run game and think our offense relies on me and Declan's connection to win.

Great for my stats.

Bad for my body and Declan's arm.

Plus, I'd love to see Rex's confidence grow a little on and off the field. So far I've noticed they've been pushing him and he's mentioned how bone tired he is night after night.

Slinging my bag over my shoulder, I walk out of the mostly empty locker room to the player's parking lot. Parked next to my Mini Cooper—the one I kept—is Rex's big red truck with him sitting in the driver's seat. I toss my bag into my car and then fold my arms and lean into his open passenger door window. "Hey, man."

"Hey." Rex blushes slightly.

"What's up?"

"I was wondering if you wanted to come over for dinner tomorrow night?"

"Is your kitchen done?"

He grins. "Yeah. The rest of the house is trashed, but the kitchen and eating area are open for business."

"I'd love to come over for dinner. What time?"

"You can come over anytime, but I figured we'd eat at five."

"Goodnight Devlin," a couple of the guys from the team call across the parking lot.

I wave high above my head and return my attention to Rex, who stiffens in his seat.

What's that about?

"Five sounds good. What can I bring?"

"I just need you. I'll take care of the rest."

"Okay," My mind is still processing the way he reacted to our teammates seeing us talking when I flash him my wide, camera-ready smile. "It's a date. See you tomorrow."

I've dated both men and women. I mean, openly dated—not whatever this is with Rex—so I know what to bring over when invited to dinner. Flowers always work for women and sometimes men. Desserts work for both. Beer or wine, too.

"This isn't rocket science," I mutter to myself while walking through the grocery store. Everything about Rex is harder, mostly because I'm not sure what this friendship between us entails, nor why we're being secretive about it. I saw the way he tensed up last night when I waved at our teammates. I'm enjoying his friendship, and yes, being teammates makes anything more than a platonic relationship tricky, but I can't continue harboring a crush without knowing where I stand.

Walking aimlessly through the store, I grab two bottles of wine—one white, one red—and a six-pack of a fall sampler from a Colorado brewery. In the kitchen area, I see a set of electric LED salt and pepper shakers I think he'll enjoy and then swing by the stationary aisle to grab a gift bag and a card.

And screw it, I grab him a potted plant perfect for the bay window in his kitchen.

Twenty minutes later, I pull into his driveway, his garage door up for me. He opens the door at the same time I pull the box of goodies off my passenger seat.

"I told you not to bring anything." He smiles and part of me wants to avoid this conversation for another night, week, lifetime. I know crushing on a man who doesn't think of me that way is dangerous, but I also don't want to shatter the blooming friendship forming either. Honestly, it's been nice having a crush, even if it's unrequited and I'm not sure I'm ready to kill it just yet.

"How could I not? My mama raised a gentleman, and I don't let someone cook for me without bringing over something. Besides—" I hand him the gift bag "—it's the first of many housewarmings, considering your new kitchen."

He takes the bag, a small blush hitting his cheeks. Man, I will never tire of that. "Thanks. Come on in."

I walk through the door to a brand new kitchen and eating area perfectly crafted. "This looks great."

"You think?" He puts the gift bag down and runs his hand over the matte black granite countertops. "I honestly had no idea what I wanted, but they came to me with a couple of designs and now I'm going to let them revamp the whole house."

I chuckle and nod my approval. "It's masculine, yet modern and chic. I like the stained concrete floors and dark countertops with wood and frosted glass cabinet doors. Is this black walnut?"

"Yeah. Wow. I'm impressed you know that."

"Stainless steel appliances and a faux brick backsplash—very nice, Rex."

"Thanks," He beams with homeowner pride. "I'm going to have them update my bedroom and bathroom next and then maybe the backyard."

"I'm glad they are working out for you." I pull out the potted plant, bottles of wine and beer from the box. "Open your gift."

He does, pulling out the card and the salt and pepper shakers. "Cool."

I lean my ass against the counter and watch him open the card. The smile on his face drops as he reads my words—words I felt divinely inspired by the mother I'll never meet.

Rex -

Congratulations on one of the many accomplishments you'll have in your life. I'm proud of

*the strides you make daily to do better, be better,
and achieve all you are meant to achieve. You're a
good man and deserve the best.*
   Your friend - Devlin

It's the confusion on his face that solidifies my decision. We have to have this conversation—tonight.

"Look, Rex. I don't want to ruin dinner or the mood or anything, but I need to talk to you about something."

He looks up with unshed tears in his eyes. "What's up?"

I rub the stubble on my jaw and sigh. "You know I'm bisexual, right?"

His lips part as time stops between us. A million thoughts run through my mind as my heart clenches and screams *don't ruin this*, but I know this has to happen. I swear, it's probably only three seconds, and yet it feels like a lifetime.

Slowly, he nods. "I'm sure I've heard or read that before."

Pursing my lips, I grab one bottle of beer and crack it open, needing the distraction. Taking a deep drink, I brace for heartbreak. "Last night, you seemed spooked that the other players knew we were talking."

Surprise morphs into confusion. "Huh? I wasn't worried if they knew I was talking to you, but I thought maybe you wouldn't want to be seen hanging out with me."

"What?" Now it's my turn to be confused.

"Well, I mean, you are you and I am me."

"That doesn't make any sense, Rex."

He shakes his head, clearly exasperated that he has to spell it out for me.

"I'm a third-string running back, second-string kick returner, and you are one of the most valuable players in the league. Not just the Rangers, but the whole league. You are up here—" he raises up on his tiptoes and puts his hand way above his head "—and I'm down here."

"So? You are taking your opportunity and running with it. Literally. I've been watching you at practice. The coaches are pushing you, testing you, and you are answering them with your very best. I see it, so I know they see it."

He glances down at the floor. "Something tells me you have something to do with their sudden interest in me."

"I will neither confirm nor deny," I make a show of locking my lips and throwing away the ky.

"That's fair," he sighs.

I take a deep breath and let it out slowly. "There's something else."

"Okay?"

"Sometimes I feel like you're flirting with me, and I guess I need to know if I'm misinterpreting things."

He shakes his head. "Devlin, I wouldn't know how to flirt if I tried."

Disappointment drops a lead ball into my gut. "I understand."

"No, I don't think you do." Rex runs his hands through his hair, his eyes cast down to the granite island between us. "I've never been in a relationship, and I'm not good at flirting. That's why none of my online dating experiences have gone past two, maybe three dates. I'm also not somebody who craves sex. As a matter of fact, I don't even think about it—except when I think about how, as a twenty-six-year-old man, I should be trying to get laid all the time. I mean, that's what guys our age are supposed to think about, right? So, if you've ever thought I was flirting with you, it wasn't because I was trying—it was natural."

"What are you saying?"

"I'm attracted to you—I mean, I think I am. How else do I explain the feelings and thoughts I have surrounding you?"

I want to close the distance between us. That's what I would normally do if someone confessed feelings for me I shared. But, I think he's telling me he's asexual, which I'm not sure how to approach.

"What thoughts, Rex?" I lean forward on the island, resting my forearms against the cool stone.

"I think you're beautiful. Smart and driven—I'm inspired by you. I look forward to seeing you every morning, even if it's from afar, and I rush home every night to log on so I don't miss you. I've opened up to you in a way I have never done with another, and completely trust that you'll take care of my thoughts and feelings, even when I don't know what kind of care I require. You are always in my thoughts, and lately, I've noticed that everything I do is in hopes you will like it. Hell—" he waves his hands over the kitchen "—it took everything within me not to ask your opinion when I picked out this decor, even though I desperately wanted your approval. Is that attraction or something else?"

"Sounds like a crush." I smile when he finally looks into my eyes. "I know because I have one on you."

"You do?"

"Yeah, man."

Rex grabs a beer and cracks it open, taking a deep drink to rival mine from a few minutes ago. "What do we do now?"

"I honestly don't know. Normally, when I'm digging on someone who feels the same way, we can't keep our hands off each other. I've never been in a relationship with a teammate."

He hangs his head. "Yeah, that's what I figured."

I step around the island, placing myself within touching distance of him. "What do you want to do?"

"I'd like that hug you promised me." Rex says after several seconds of contemplative silence.

I chuckle and open my arms wide. "I've been waiting for you to say that for weeks."

He takes a tentative step toward me and I close the distance, wrapping my arms around him and pulling him tight against my chest. There's a moment of awkwardness and then he melts against me, letting out a deep sigh. "It's been a long time since someone hugged me."

"How long?" I tighten my arms and rest my face in the crook of his neck, basking in his warmth, reveling in the feel of his hard, muscular chest.

"A few months before my mom died." He slides his

palm up my back, his breath tickling my jaw. "This is nice."

I pull my face back to look him in the eye. Our mouths are so close, our breaths mingle. "My hugs are available to you anytime you like."

"I'm sorry I'm not any good at this," he whispers.

"We don't have to do anything you don't want to do."

"What if I want more?"

Ever so slowly, I lean forward, letting my actions speak for me. Rex's lips part and he closes his eyes the moment mine touch his—wordlessly giving himself to me and this moment. His mouth is soft and his tongue is slick as I slide mine against his, tasting him for the first time. Electricity jolts through my body as every nerve ending wakes up, letting me know this is real—this is happening. I run my hands up his back and cup either side of his neck, deepening the kiss when he moans his pleasure. He fists the back of my shirt and presses the length of his body against mine at the same time I trail kisses along his jaw and nibble on his earlobe.

"Mmmm," I groan in his ear. "Better than I dreamed."

"You've dreamed about kissing me?" Rex pants.

"For weeks. Maybe longer." I pull back and give him a reassuring smile. "You okay?"

He nods. "I was afraid that would never happen."

"Anytime you want a hug or a kiss from me, claim it."

"Are you hungry?" He drops his hands and takes a step back.

"Starved," I say, meaning every interpretation of the

word and knowing that while I want more, I'm willing to wait until he's ready. Honestly, I'm thankful the conversation went so well.

He smirks, letting me know he gets my meaning. "Grab a seat and I'll bring the first course to you."

Chapter 6
Rex

After serving Devlin a three-course meal, starting with salad and ending with crème brûlée, we retire to my living room and sit side by side on the loveseat between my two recliners. "Want to watch a movie?"

"I'd like that." Devlin crosses his legs at the ankle and stretches his arm over the back of the cushion.

I grab the remote and turn on the TVs, engaging dual-screen and flipping through the newest movies available for rent. "Action, fantasy, horror?"

We both chuckle as I stop on the new Dungeons and Dragons movie.

"Have you seen it yet?" Devlin's voice is smooth velvet near my ear and it sends a shiver down my spine, even though he isn't touching me.

"Not yet. You?" I turn to look into his beautiful eyes, which are currently a golden color.

"No," He shakes his head, his eyes dropping to my mouth.

Without overthinking it, I lean forward and press my lips to his, wanting this as much as I think he does. He slides his big hand into my hair, controlling the kiss even though I'm the one pinning him down by pushing my body against his. Within minutes, we're kissing passionately, the tentativeness from earlier gone. I'm not sure if I climbed onto his lap, or if he pulled me in place, but I'm straddling his lap, my hands gripping his biceps while his fingers dig into the tops of my thighs. His groans and growls as he kisses my neck and sucks on my collarbone sends blood rushing to my dick.

"I like kissing you." He flexes his hands against my quads, massaging me, but not venturing near my groin.

"I like kissing you," I reply lamely, unable to think of something better to say and wishing I didn't find sex and intimacy so uncomfortable.

"We should slow down. I don't want you to do anything you're not ready to do."

"I'm not a virgin, Devlin."

He raises his brow. "You've been with a man before?"

"Yes, kind of."

"Maybe you should explain."

"All of my experiences were in my sophomore year in college. My roommate was bisexual, as was his girlfriend, and they were very experimental. They were so wild and free that I envied them sometimes. The three of us played together a few times. Sometimes, he and I would play by ourselves."

"Did you like it?"

"I did." I bite my lip. "It's not that I don't like sex, it's that I don't think about it much. I'm not driven by the need to get off, if that makes sense."

"It makes sense." Devlin runs his fingers through my hair and smiles softly. "I'm content kissing and holding you like this."

"And if I want to touch you?"

His smile widens. "Baby, you can touch me any way you want."

Slowly, tentatively, I slide my hands down his hard chest, perfectly honed by hard work and good genes. He rests his hands on my upper thighs, his thumbs pressing hot little circles near my groin. We're both wearing loose-fitting joggers and our erections are evident. Gathering up the hem of his shirt, I coax him to raise his arms over his head and pull the fabric free. I've seen him shirtless plenty of times in the locker room, but this is different. This is intimate and only for me.

"To quote *Men's Fitness* magazine, you have a beautiful body." I slide my hand tenderly over his pectoral muscles, his skin prickling and forming goosebumps, his nipples hardening into tight little buds.

"Take your shirt off, Rex. Let me admire you while you touch me." Devlin's voice is hoarse and strained, and the raspy request turns me on a bit more.

I pull my shirt off and throw it on the recliner next to his. He lifts his hands, sliding them up my arms to wrap them gently around my neck. "I love your freckles. I want to kiss every single one."

"I have them all over."

He hisses, pulling my face to his, his lips hovering over mine. "Don't tease me."

I didn't mean to tease or flirt, but I'm glad it came across that way. Moaning, I slide my hands down his stomach which is more rippled eight-pack than flat, and brush my palm over the head of his erection. Devlin groans deep in his throat but doesn't stop his tongue's exploration of my mouth. He kisses me thoroughly until rational thought no longer prevails and the only thing left between us is raw desire.

I grip Devlin through his nylon pants, wrapping my fingers tightly around his cock. Memories of Tim going down on me or me going down on him flood to the surface, reminding me how good it feels to touch and be touched by another.

Pulling back to break our kiss, I stare into Devlin's beautiful eyes, which are nearly black with arousal. "Can I?"

I don't have to complete my thoughts. He nods slowly. "If you want to."

"I want to."

He slides his hands down my arms and back to my thighs, this time whisking his fingertips over my erection. "I want to, too."

A devilish smirk curls my lips as bratty words leave my mouth. "Me first."

I push back off his lap and drop to my knees between his splayed thighs. He helps me free his erection from his joggers, pre-cum glistening on the tip. I wrap my fingers around his soft heat and use my thumb to spread his arousal.

Devlin draws in a deep breath, shifting his hips and leaning his head back.

"Do me a favor?" I say before running my tongue from base to tip.

"What's that, baby?"

"If you like it, let me hear it." I glance up to see him look down at me. "I want to hear your pleasure."

He smiles and nods. "You got it."

It's been a long time, but you never forget how good a hot, wet, soft mouth feels, and while I enjoy having my dick sucked, there's something about controlling someone else's pleasure with such a simple act that is addicting. I take him as deep as I can, coating him in my saliva, my fist lazily stroking his shaft as I take my time getting to know what he likes and what he loves.

Devlin lets out another ragged breath, this time groaning as my thumb presses against the sensitive ridge near the head. "That feels so good."

Each gasp and groan eggs me on while the occasional curse word barking from his lips has my hard-on weeping pre-cum. I take his cock deep and stroke him hard, then worship the head by swirling my tongue and gently scraping my bottom teeth over the sensitive bundle of nerves. It doesn't take long before Devlin has one palm resting against my cheek, the other fisting the back of my hair, his hips coming up as his body grows tight. "Fuck, baby. I'm going to come."

I've never swallowed before, but I want to make

Devlin happy. He decides for me by pulling me off him, leaning forward and kissing me hard. His intensity has me climbing onto the couch to straddle his lap once again. Without preamble, he takes my hand and wraps it around his cock while using his other hand to slide into my pants and free my hard-on.

He strokes me, growling as he thrusts his hips up into my hand. "You feel so good, Rex,"

I wrap my free hand around the back of his neck, letting myself go to the pleasure shooting up my spine. He touches me with such intimate knowledge, it's like I'm stroking myself. Only this way I see the desire dancing in his eyes as he's on the brink of releasing.

He's so damn beautiful.

"I want to wait for you, but I can't," he roars at the same time he orgasms, his cum shooting out in thick pearly ropes onto his chest. His fist is wrapped around me, although he doesn't move—his body wired tight as his cock jumps in four successive spurts. Finally, he relaxes and pants for breath, looking into my eyes for something.

"Are you okay?"

I nod. "That was amazing."

Languidly, he slides his hand up and down my shaft. "Will you come for me?"

I close my eyes for a second, blocking out the reality of what we're doing and let myself enjoy his touch. It's been so long since I've last come, it doesn't take long for the pressure to build in my balls.

Devlin pulls me close and kisses me tenderly. "Tell me how you like it, baby."

"Just like that." I moan, leaning my forehead against his. "Oh damn, that feels good."

"Has it really been since your sophomore year that another person has touched you?" Devlin tightens his grip and strokes me a little harder, making me come onto his stomach in five short strokes.

Nodding, I grip his forearm, panting and begging him to stop. "Yes."

Devlin releases my cock and looks down at our cum on his chest and then brings his eyes up to mine. He swipes his thumb over my cheek and then pulls my lips to his. "I'm glad you waited for me."

I feel like there's a lot more meaning behind those words, but I don't know that either of us can investigate them now. "I'll get you a towel."

Climbing off his lap, I tuck myself back into my joggers and duck into the spare bathroom, washing my hands and running a washcloth under the warm water. Back in the living room, I lean over him and wipe the evidence of our passion off his chest. Devlin takes the washcloth from me and pulls me down beside him.

"Are you okay?" His face is a mask of concern as he brushes my hair back from my forehead.

"I'm good." I nod. And I am—I feel great—even though I'm not sure what this all means in the grand scheme of things. We're not just two random guys who dig each other, we're teammates. What will the players think? The organization? The league or the public at large? I don't know if there are any openly gay football players, much less couples playing for the same team.

"I really like you, Rex, so it's important to me you are comfortable with this—with us. I don't want things to get weird."

Frowning, I grab his hand and kiss his fingertips. "What is this?"

"The progression of our friendship and the start of a relationship—I hope." He interlaces our fingers to hold my hand.

"How do we handle this and the team?"

Devlin sighs and adjusts his position on the couch, pressing his back against the corner and spreading his arms over the tops of the cushions. "Although I've never denied being bisexual, I don't advertise my dating life. It's nobody's damn business who I date."

Our knees touch and I slide my free hand around his calf. I need to touch him as we have this difficult conversation. Honestly, I'm not ready to put my tenuous position on the team at risk, and I'm sure if we were public, it would be. It's not like the team would risk losing him. He's one of the main reasons we have a shot at the championship. "Are you worried about how our teammates will react?"

He shakes his head. "No. I trust them to be cool, but considering the organization wants us to avoid scandal this season, I'm thinking we keep this on the down-low until we know where this is going."

"Okay." I nod my agreement.

"But—" he hooks his finger under my chin and grips my jaw, his thumb brushing tenderly over my bottom lip

"—if you want to shout it from the rooftops, I'm down with that, too."

Heat burns my cheeks. Even though I would love that, some part of me knows it is an impossibility. Walking hand-in-hand into the locker room or the classroom would cause a riot, right? At the very least team management would definitely call it *shenanigans*. "I think it would be best to keep this between us for now."

Devlin checks his watch. "We have enough time to watch half of a movie before curfew, and I'd really like to cuddle on the couch before I leave."

"I'd like that, too."

Chapter 7
Devlin

After our second loss of the season, the mood in the locker room is dour. The coaches and GM come into the room, but I'm not sure anyone is interested in hearing them.

"We expected today's game to be our toughest of the season. Seattle is the team to beat this year, but I know we are fundamentally better than them in every position. I bear the blame for this loss, and should have seen this coming after our loss to Philly two weeks ago," Mike Monroe says calmly.

Daniel Scott steps forward. "No, Mike. We're a team, a family, and the front office has been holding on too tightly. That's my fault. You guys need a break. Over a month ago, I asked for your best and I feel you've been giving it. Today is a reflection of what happens when it's all work and no play. We are all wound tight, and you need some time to cut loose and relax. Effective immediately, the team curfew is lifted and Monday family days are reinstated. We're still going from seven to seven Wednesday through Sunday, but I'm hoping you can decompress without ending up in jail or as headline fodder."

Mike Monroe nods. "You guys are doing a great job. Today was a bad day. Take a few days off, decompress, and come back ready to dominate on Wednesday."

I glance across the locker room at Rex as everyone chats amongst themselves. Darren is waiting for me in the player's parking lot, and I desperately want to invite Rex to join us. Now that the curfew and restrictions are lifted, I wonder if he'd be down with catching a later flight with me tomorrow?

Rex, Jepson, and Jaxson are talking... no, actually, it looks like Jepson and Jaxson are bickering while Rex tries to keep up, but he steals a glance in my direction and I casually throw him a wink in return. It's only been a few days since we fooled around at his house, but we haven't had time to be alone since. That night I fell asleep on the couch with him in my arms and didn't make it home until early morning. It was my best night in a long time.

I tap Aggie's shoulder and grab my bag. "I'll see you tomorrow night."

Aggie nods, a nice smile spreading on his lips. Ever since his divorce was finalized a few days ago, the man seems a hundred pounds lighter. "Yeah, man. Have a nice time with your brother."

Walking toward the doors, I glance in Rex's direction one last time, but he's got his head in his bag. Not wanting to be obvious and get caught looking at my teammate all moony-eyed, I duck out of the locker room and walk ten feet down the hall to where Declan and Deacon are talking to my brother.

Deacon and my brother are close to the same age and played ball against each other when Darren was a rookie—meeting briefly a handful of times before the fateful injury that took Deacon out of the game nearly six years ago. Darren was playing for the Denver Mustangs at the time—his first team out of college—alongside his teammate, Rylie Reynolds, who coincidentally is the one who took Deacon out with a defensive quarterback sack.

Darren playing for Denver was the whole reason I had my heart set on playing for a Colorado team during the draft, but he got traded to Seattle last season. Still, we try to sneak an extra day or two whenever one of us visits the other person's city.

I join the trio, making sure I'm facing the locker room doors so I can see Rex as he's leaving. I know it will raise questions, but I want to—no, I have to—introduce him to my brother.

Seconds later, Jaxson walks out, his gait long and purposeful as he passes us. Ten seconds after that, Jepson and Rex also walk out.

As if he can feel me, Rex's eyes immediately come to me. I wait until he gets closer and then softly call his name. Of course, Jepson also stops.

"Hey, man. I want to introduce you to my brother," I say casually to both of them, even though this was not the plan.

Jepson smiles and offers his hand while Rex blushes slightly before also offering his.

"Gentlemen." Darren clasps both of their hands while Deacon and Declan say their goodbyes, leaving the four of us in an awkward circle.

Thankfully, Jepson is a born talker and engages my brother quickly about living in Seattle, giving me a tiny window to pull Rex aside. "What do you think about ditching the ride home and staying here with me tonight?"

He smiles coyly. "That sounds amazing but would be super obvious. Don't you think so?"

I sigh. "Maybe. Probably. You could tell the coach that now that the lockdown is lifted, you want to stay the night and visit an old girlfriend."

Turning my back to Jepson and Darren, I let my fingertips brush against Rex's arm.

He sucks in his breath. "I can't, Devlin. I don't have the good favor with the team to risk any perceived trouble."

He's right. I know he's right. And I don't begrudge him for protecting his career, even if I don't agree with his perception of how things will go down. Maybe I'm a fool, but I have more faith in my teammates and the organization than Rex does. Then again, the team isn't going to risk losing me while they have their eye on a championship ring. As he said, he doesn't have the pull I do. "Okay."

"You come home tomorrow, right?" he says lowly, his dark eyes searching mine.

"Yeah, but it'll be late."

"That's okay. Come to my house. I'll text you the code to my garage."

I give him a small, knowing smile. "I'll message you later tonight."

Rex clears his throat and takes a small step back at the same time Jepson finally takes a breath.

"You guys better catch your bus." I tilt my head to the parking lot.

Jepson nods, and once again shakes my brother's hand. "It was nice to meet you, Darren."

"Have a nice dinner." Rex nods, meeting my brother's eyes only for a second.

My brother has a knowing glint in his eye as he grabs hold of Rex's hand and doesn't immediately let go. "It was nice to meet you, Rex. Hopefully, we'll get a chance to meet again soon."

Rex blushes ever so slightly and casts his eyes to the ground. "That would be nice."

I wait until they are on the bus before smacking my brother on the shoulder. "What the hell was that?"

"How long has this been going on?" He looks at me, shakes his head and walks to his car, leaving me to follow him like the little brother that I am.

"How can you tell?"

"Little bro, I can always tell when you're crushing on someone. Do your teammates know?"

"No. Not yet. It's new and we're trying to figure it out."

He chuckles low under his breath. "Yeah, but you

like him—a lot—and I'd garner a guess that he likes you, too. How adorable is he with those freckles and blushing red cheeks?"

"Irresistible." I slump into the passenger seat of his big SUV, two car seats that house my niece and nephew in the passenger row behind me. "I've never crushed on a teammate before, and I don't know how to handle this. You know me. I've never hidden my feelings for anyone."

"No. Your desire to love openly and hard is one of your best characteristics, Devlin. Is he closeted?"

"No. Yes. I'm not really sure. He's never been in a relationship with a woman or a man."

"That seems hard to believe. He's so cute."

I narrow my eyes. My brother is one hundred percent straight and married with two kids. "Are you fucking with me?"

He laughs. "Of course not. But I know you. Hiding your feelings is going to eat away at you after a while. You're the holding hands, flower-giving, romantic type. I bet not being able to touch him right now just about killed you."

I snort. "You have no idea, but even if he was openly gay or bisexual, with a championship season on the line, we don't want to bring any unnecessary attention to ourselves or our relationship. Not right now."

"I understand that." He nods, turning out of traffic into an underground garage. "I'm sure you will work it out, whatever it takes. Is he good to you?"

Smiling, I unfasten my seatbelt. "He's sweet, kind of shy, and starved for connection. He lost his mom a few years ago and doesn't have any other family to speak of. The team brought him on mid-season last year, but we met at a gaming shop a month ago and started talking."

"Oh... that makes sense. He's a geek, too." My brother wraps his hand around the back of my neck and squeezes.

"So are you, if you ever took the time to log on."

"Man, I don't have time between practice, Patrice, and the kids." He hops out of the SUV, and I follow him to the garage entrance of a nice restaurant. Tonight it's just the two of us, but I'm hanging out with the whole family tomorrow at the pier until my flight in the evening.

The eyes of the guy waiting at the hostess stand bug out when he sees us. "The Frank brothers! Do you think I can get a picture?"

We both shrug. "Sure."

The guy hands his bewildered girlfriend his phone and lifts on his tiptoes with his arms around our shoulders, and I'm thankful Rex isn't here right now. A random photo hitting Instagram picturing us on a night on the town might give us away. Or maybe not. I know I'd feel guilty considering all the thoughts running through my head. He said he doesn't think about sex, but I haven't been able to stop thinking about touching and tasting him again.

But mostly, I want to wake up with him in my arms. That was too nice to not crave it on a daily basis.

"Thanks, guys. Sorry about your loss tonight—" the guy tilts his head in my direction "—but go Seattle!"

I chuckle and roll my eyes while my brother laughs and says, "We all know my brother is dominating the league right now, so this win tonight is extra special to me."

"I have two brothers, so I understand sibling rivalries." The guy shakes Darren's hand.

The restaurant owner rushes over to save us before more fans clamor for a picture. "Mr. Frank, your table is this way."

After we settle with our drinks in hand, my brother leans back against the booth and stares at me. "You should bring Rex to Thanksgiving."

I choke on my Old Fashioned. "That's a month away."

He shrugs. "If you two are still going strong by then—and he has no family, as you said—I think it would be nice to introduce him to our crazy crew and give him a sense of belonging, even if it is only for a couple of days."

Rolling my eyes, I shake my head and divert the conversation to him. "How's Patrice doing?"

He smiles and nods, understanding my need to process everything before committing to anything. My brother knows me well, and he knows I don't do casual. I've had a handful of relationships in my life, most lasting six months or longer, and every one of them has met some or all of my family members. Sure, there have been a dozen crazy nights when it was all about sex and exploration, but otherwise, I'm a committed kind of guy.

Which, as Darren aptly pointed out, is why a secret relationship with my teammate is going to grate on me over time. But it's crazy to be thinking about it now considering we just stepped over the friendship line into something more.

"She's good—" Darren says, breaking me out of my thoughts "—and excited to see you."

"I'm excited to see them, too." I nod at the server as they deliver our food. We spend the rest of the meal talking about our parents, the "it" Christmas presents this year, and lastly about my new Mini Cooper, which Darren predictably clowns me for as he pulls into his driveway.

"Get Rex to take a picture of you sitting in it and send it to me. It's going on our Christmas card."

"Fuck you." I chuckle, surprised when the garage door flies open and two small children run out. "I thought they'd be asleep."

"They are supposed to be. I guess they were too excited waiting for you."

"Now I feel bad. We should have come straight here and grabbed a snack." I slide out of the passenger seat and sneak around the front of the hood to surprise my niece and nephew.

"Daddy! Where's Uncle D?" I hear Vanessa ask.

"I don't know." My brother shrugs but stares right at me. "He was just here. You better find him."

"Rawr!" I jump up, causing both of them to squeal and run at me full speed. Swooping them up into my arms, I pepper both of their faces with kisses and carry them into the house. "Hi, Patrice."

"Hi, Devlin."

"Sorry we woke up the babies." I plant a kiss on her cheek.

"They refused to go to bed until their Uncle D was home to tuck them in." She rolls her eyes but gives me a warm smile.

After tucking them in, I bid my brother and his wife goodnight and climb into bed with my phone in hand. Rex got home an hour ago and texted me.

> 5:47 PM - I hope you're not upset that I said no to staying. I wanted to, but it scared me to say yes. My feelings for you… I can't quite explain them. Regardless, I can't wait to see you tomorrow night. My garage code is 101221 and I'll leave the door to the house unlocked. Let yourself in. I think I'm going to Denver with the twins tomorrow night for a birthday dinner and maybe a club. Text me once you get on the plane and I will be home close to the time you arrive.

> 9:32 PM - I'm not upset. Honestly, it was impetuous for me to ask. I understand about the feelings—I have some intense ones going on myself, but we can talk about it more tomorrow night. I can't wait to hold you in my arms again. Even though I've seen you every day, I miss you. Tomorrow, my brother, sister-in-law and I are taking the kids down to the pier. Have you been? Text me when you get home so I know you're safe.

9:33 PM - I just pulled into my driveway. We made record time flying home. I spent the entire trip wishing I had the balls to say yes and stay with you tonight. No, I've never been to Seattle outside of playing football. Is it nice?

Don't beat yourself up for not staying. Honestly, Seattle is not my favorite city, nor is it Darren's, but it's where they live for now. Pike Place Market is interesting, or at least a novelty. Tomorrow I will drink coffee and eat tiny powdered donuts because that's what the kids will want, and then we're taking them to the aquarium. Regardless, I'd love to bring you here sometime.

I'd like that.

Talk to you tomorrow, baby. Sleep well.

You too.

I set my phone down with a sense of longing filling my chest. In a little over twenty-four hours, I will have Rex in my arms again—my world settled for another day.

How did I become attached to him so quickly, and what will I do if his feelings don't run as deep as mine?

Chapter 8
Rex

I play it cool with Jepson, Jaxson, and Rylie—acting like I have nowhere to be—but on the inside, I'm clawing my way home. As it is, a bit of drama gets me out of the club early. Even though Rylie's nanny is a great girl from a small town like mine, I'm secretly counting every mile marker we pass on the way home.

Fifteen minutes ago, I got a text from Devlin letting me know he arrived at my house and let himself in. I told him I was on I-25, heading his way. This excitement rumbling in my stomach is new, and the idea of me coming home to someone is surreal.

I say goodbye to Sunshine and Rylie, casting my teammate a *we will be talking about this later* look—even though it is none of my business—and wait until they are out of sight to open my garage to reveal Devlin's Mini Cooper.

The downstairs bathroom door opens at the same time I lock the door behind me, steam billowing out of the small room to reveal an Adonis wrapped in navy blue terry cloth.

I don't know why, but a blush hits my cheeks as parts of my body warm up. "Hey."

"Hi." Devlin smiles. "I hope you don't mind me using your shower."

"Of course not. What's mine is yours."

"How much longer until they finish your primary bedroom and bathroom remodel?"

"A couple of weeks. They've already ripped out the old shower liner and cabinets."

"I can't wait to see it." Devlin approaches slowly and wraps one arm around my waist, pulling my body against his. He kisses me softly, his eyes closed, savoring the moment—and me. "God, I feel like I've waited a lifetime to kiss you again."

Leaning my forehead against his, I smile. "Yeah."

He pats my ass and then lets me go, walking back into the bedroom where his bag is to grab a pair of shorts. With his back to me, he drops his towel and slips on his shorts, much like he would in the locker room. "How was your night?"

I kick off my shoes and unfasten my belt, pulling my shirttails out of my slacks. "It was weird."

Devlin sits on the edge of the bed and pulls me to stand in front of him. He glances up at me and meticulously unfastens the buttons on my shirt. "Tell me about it."

It's empowering to watch a strong, powerful man tend to me, and my need to reach out and stroke his cheek is overwhelming. "Well, first we took Jepson and Jaxson's girlfriend to dinner and then to a strip club."

His brow arches. "*Their* girlfriend?"

"Yeah." I don't want to gossip about my friends, but how can I not?

"Interesting." He peels open my shirt and slides the fabric off my shoulders.

"And then Rylie's nanny—who he caught dancing on stage tonight—drove us home, but he refused to talk and made me sit in the front seat next to her."

"I take it he didn't know she worked there?"

I shake my head, my breath catching when Devlin presses his lips to my lower stomach. "No."

"Hmmmm—drama abounds. I hope they work it out because I know finding a good nanny has been stressful for Rylie."

"Me too. She seems like a nice girl."

Devlin rests his chin above my navel and looks up at me with his big hands wrapped around my waist, his hazel eyes glittering with mischief. "Want to climb into bed?"

"If that's what you want." I'm panting, and he hasn't touched me yet.

"I could tell you what I want, but I don't want to push you into anything."

"Tell me." I wrap my hands around his neck and caress his jaw with my thumbs.

"I desperately want to taste you on my tongue."

Biting my lip, I nod slowly. "You can touch and taste me however you like."

Flashing me his million-dollar smile, he pulls back as his fingers deftly pop the button on my slacks and glide down the zipper. My pants sag low on my hips and he slides his palm over my growing erection, growling low in his throat. "I've been dreaming about touching and tasting you since Wednesday morning. I never meant for us to fall asleep and hoped to play some more before the movie ended."

He pushes my boxers down and wraps his lips around my semi-hard cock. Devlin moans, sending vibrations up my shaft and to my balls.

My eyes flutter closed, and my fingertips flex on the back of his neck as I give myself over to the pleasure coursing through my body. It takes nothing for me to grow fully erect as Devlin takes me deep, working my length and coating me in his saliva before popping me free from his hot, hungry mouth. "You have a nice dick, baby. I want to worship him, and you, until the morning light."

I'm not sure how to reply to that other than begging him to make it true. Instead, I answer with a pleasing hum from my lips. "That feels amazing."

He uses one hand to stroke while cupping, kneading, and tugging on my balls softly with the other. Although we've only touched each other once before, he seems to know I like a gentler hand, and it doesn't take long before I'm digging my fingers into his shoulders, panting my restraint, and yet desperate to let go.

"Devlin?" I beg in desperation.

"Yes, baby?" He pulls back, running his tongue along the underside of my shaft and looking up at me.

Fuck, I don't think I've ever seen anything more beautiful. "I'm close."

"I know. I'm going to make you come hard for me."

Devlin's confidence in everything he does is intoxicating. I want to bask in his strength and absorb a little for myself.

He opens his mouth wide and takes me deep, sucking while using the tip of his fingers to massage my perineum. Any control I think I have over my orgasm disintegrates as my cock jerks and cum shoots out of my shaft.

"Oh, fuck," I hiss and grip his shoulders, unable to control myself.

Devlin continues, the wet sound of him slurping turning me on in a whole new way. I push him off me and drop to my knees, my pants still tangled around my ankles. "I want to please you, too."

"You will—" he stops me from pulling off his towel "—but with your naked body pressed against mine. Come up on the bed, baby."

Groaning, I stand up and kick my pants and socks off while he crawls up the bed and pulls down the comforter, sliding his gloriously naked form beneath the sheets. "I like when you call me baby."

He grins, crooking his finger and beckoning me to lie beside him. "And I like calling you baby."

"What pet name should I call you?"

Devlin takes care to tug the covers up to my waist, and then he pulls me into his arms and hoists my leg up over his hip. "I don't know. That's up to you to figure out."

"Why does this—you and I—feel so natural? I'm almost twenty-six years old and no interaction has ever felt so... right." I run my thumb over his lips and then lean forward to kiss him, not waiting for an answer. How could Devlin explain me to me, anyway? He's had plenty of relationships and, just like on the field, knows how to be who, what, and where his partner needs. Is this effortless for we him too, or is he holding himself back to accommodate my idiosyncrasies?

His cock is hard and pressed against my belly as we kiss with the kind of passion longstanding lovers have for each other. He glides his fingers into my hair and slides his knee between my legs, rolling his hips to rub his erection against my inner thigh. The friction is erotic and consuming. I slip my hand between us and wrap my fingers around him, encouraging him to fuck my fist.

He growls low in his throat and nips at my bottom lip. "It feels natural because deep down, on some cosmic level, we were looking for each other. I thought you were hot the first time I saw you, but I've never dated a teammate. Honestly, I thought it was impossible. But when you asked me about threesomes in Nashville... it opened a floodgate I could no longer ignore. Then, running into you at the game shop solidified my truth. I can't resist you."

Devlin rolls me to my back, settling his weight between my splayed legs, and proceeds to kiss me breathlessly. "Can I ask you a question, baby?"

"Yes." I slide my hands down his sides to his hips.

"What is this to you? Are we experimenting? Playing around? Friends with benefits?"

"I thought we were going to keep this between us for now." My brow furrows. Where is he going with this? Does he want to tell our teammates about us already?

"For now, yes. But I'm wondering if there can be a future for us, or is that completely out of the question for you?" His eyes are a deep forest green as he stares back into mine, looking for the answer I can't give. I've never been in a relationship. I wouldn't even know what that looked like for me.

"Could you be in a relationship with someone like me?" I ask tentatively.

"Yes," he says without hesitation.

His answer fills me with joy. "I've never been in one, but I will tell you that the idea of seeing you tonight filled me with a kind of excitement I've never felt before. I wanted nothing more than to wrap up my night, come home, and sink into your arms."

Devlin smiles and kisses me softly. "That's good, baby. That's real good."

He adjusts himself, pressing his dick to mine, then rolls his hips against my lower belly. "Can you come again for me?"

I nod. "Yes."

Devlin kisses me and then moves his perfect body up on his knees. "Bring your legs up, Rex."

My eyes bug out a little. "Uh, Devlin, I've never done that."

He stares at me for a second, and then I see understanding smooth his features. "We aren't doing that tonight, baby. I have something else in mind."

Pulling my legs up, Devlin kisses my knee and positions himself so our dicks align. Then he grabs my hand and wraps it around our cocks, controlling my grip with his hand. Together we stroke each other and ourselves, hardening in our partner's grasp until we're both panting and on the verge of coming. At some point, we let go and grab onto each other, jerking our hands to bring our lover pleasure. Devlin leans over me to claim my mouth as we both grunt and groan through our release, shooting cum onto our stomachs.

We stare into each other's eyes, unspoken words of love and devotion filling the silent space unheard over our heavy breathing. His eyes glitter, the gold specks making them dance. "I'll grab a towel."

Leaving me in bed, he comes back sixty seconds later with a warm cloth, cleaning me and then himself. "Ready for bed?"

I nod. "I am."

Even though we are in my room, Devlin hits the switch on the wall and plunges us into darkness. He feels his way to the bed, slipping underneath the sheets and pulling me to his chest. "Do you normally sleep on your back or your side?"

"Both." I snuggle into the crook of his arm and rest my cheek against his hard chest. "I think I know what pet name I'll give you."

"What's that?" He runs his fingers up and down my arm lovingly.

"Like in the fantasy realms we run our characters through, you are my king. I might not know how to be in a relationship, but I know I am yours to do with as you please because all I want to do is please you."

He kisses the top of my head. "If I am your king, Rex, then you are my prince. Mine to care for, mine to shower with affection, mine to love."

It seems absurd to talk about this, and yet I know he's right. I feel it deep in my soul. "Yours."

"Mine." He agrees.

Chapter 9
Devlin

For the past three weeks, Rex and I have been sneaking around, stealing moments on the road, and spending a couple nights each week in his bed. We cook, game, snuggle, and talk, and somehow have kept our relationship a secret. I think the reason behind our success is that everyone else seems to have their own things going on.

Declan found out he's the father of a cute five-year-old, and he's working on rekindling the relationship with the mother of his child. Aggie's divorce is final, and he's in the process of moving out of my basement and into Declan's sky-rise apartment. Jepson and Jaxson are dating a woman, so their nights are occupied, which leaves Rex and my evenings free.

With Thanksgiving rapidly approaching—now that I know this isn't a fling—it is time to invite Rex to my brother's house to meet my family.

"I want you to come to Seattle with me on Wednesday night," I blurt.

Rex brings his head up from the vegetables he's sautéing. "What?"

"What else are you going to do for Thanksgiving?"

"I don't know." He shrugs. "Jepson and Jaxson invited me over."

I walk up behind him and slide my arms around his waist, resting my chin on his shoulder. "My family wants to meet you."

He side-eyes me. "Do you think that's a good idea?"

"Why wouldn't it be? We may not have told our friends, but my family knows about us."

"Meeting your parents is a big deal. What if they don't like me?" he murmurs.

I squeeze him tight. "Are you kidding me? They are going to love you."

Rex sighs. "I've never met somebody's family before."

"We'll stay in a hotel nearby. That way, we have some privacy and a place to escape to if you need it. We'll hang out with them for the day, go see the sights, and fly home Friday night."

Rex turns the burner down and spins in my arms to face me. "You know I'm crazy about you, and I am beyond touched that you want me to spend the holiday with your family."

"Is that a yes?"

He grins. "That is definitely a yes."

Thursday morning, we wake up and shower together before driving to my brother's house. Patrice and my mom have been cooking since yesterday, baking bread and pies and all the goodies. Rex is fidgeting in the passenger seat of our rental when I reach over the console and slide my hand onto his thigh. "Are you going to be okay?"

"I can't believe how nervous I am."

"My family is super chill. I let them know I was bi when I was fifteen, and they've been okay with it since day one."

"I'm not nervous about that. I just want to make a good impression."

"Baby—" I pull into Darren's driveway and turn off the engine, sliding my hands onto either side of his face "—be yourself and they will love you, just like I do."

The words slip out, but I don't regret them. Rex sucks in his breath and nods. "Okay."

I pull his face to mine and give him a gentle kiss. "Ready?"

"Yes."

The front door opens, and the kids run out with my mom waiting for us in the doorway. I scoop my niece up in my arms and slow down to grab my nephew, who climbs me like a tree.

"Rex, this is my niece and nephew, Vanessa and Pablo.

Can you say hi to my friend?" I kiss both of their cheeks. Predictably, as soon as Rex smiles and shakes their little hands, Vanessa opens her arms and demands he hold her.

"Oh." Rex accepts the little girl in his arms.

"Are you Uncle D's boyfriend?" she asks with a child's innocence.

"Uh, yes?"

"Come on, y'all," my mom calls to us from the doorway.

I grab Rex's free hand and lead him to the door, each of us carrying a toddler in our arms. "Mama, this is Rex."

"It's so nice to meet you." She flashes him a warm smile.

"I see where Devlin gets his million-dollar smile," Rex says, dropping my hand to shake hers.

"I'm a hugger, sweetie." She pushes his hand away and wraps her arm around his waist, pulling him and Vanessa into a group hug and then escorts him inside, calling to the rest of the family, "They're here."

Darren and my dad come out of the TV room at the same time we set the kids down. "Rex, this is my dad, Gary, and you met Darren a few weeks ago."

"Nice to meet you." My father and Rex shake hands.

"Glad you came." Darren follows suit.

"Thanks for inviting me."

I give my mom and dad a hug and then slap palms with my brother.

"The game is on." Darren tilts his head to the TV room as if there is nothing more to say.

"Let me introduce Rex to Patrice and then we'll meet you in there." I slide my hand onto Rex's back and guide him into the kitchen where Patrice is knee-deep in serving dishes, my mother following us in.

"Smells delicious, Patrice."

"Hey, D." She looks up with a big smile and wipes her hands on a towel. "You must be Rex."

"Yes, ma'am." He shakes her hand, and the nervousness rolling off him makes me want to wrap my arms around him and hold tight.

"Oh, please call me Patrice or Patty or hey you—anything other than ma'am. I'm not old enough for that yet." She giggles.

"Patrice." He motions to the pots and pans. "Can we help you?"

"I hear you are quite the cook, but I'm pretty territorial of my kitchen on the holiday meals." She eyes the chaos meaningfully.

Rex holds his hands up. "I get it."

"You two grab a drink and check on the game. Kickoff was a few minutes ago. Can you take this to Dad?" She hands me a bowl of dip.

"Sure." I tilt my head and Rex follows me to the TV room, but let's be honest, this is a football house and there is a TV in every room. Even when we sit down to eat in a few hours, there will be a muted TV on in the dining room.

Detroit is playing Chicago on the big screen. My dad sits in one of four theater-style recliners with a small table between each seat, his eyes practically glued to the big screen.

"Hey Rex, sit beside me." My dad pats the empty chair.

Chuckling, I roll my eyes. "What do you want to drink?"

Rex shrugs. "I'll have whatever you're having."

Locking eyes with him, I give him a soft smile and a wink, attempting to reassure him that this is a safe place and he can relax. He visibly inhales and then lets it out slowly, sinking into the chair next to my dad.

At the back of the room, I fix us a couple of whiskey sours.

My brother walks up with Pablo in his arms and whispers, "Is he okay?"

"He's nervous. It's his first time meeting parents."

"Ah." Darren nods. "Mom will break him of that in no time."

"Right?" I chuckle.

The four of us settle in front of the TV, intent on the game until the commercial break, which always seems to wake us up out of our zombie state.

"So, Rex, which college did you play for?" My father asks as my mother sits on his lap, snatching a cherry tomato off his veggie plate and popping it into her mouth.

"I went to Nebraska for a couple of years, sir." He glances at me sitting on the floor with Vanessa as she colors us a picture.

"Ah yes, the Huskers. How was that?"

He shrugs. "They have a good program, but I got little playtime as a freshman or sophomore."

"That's right—" my mom says softly "—you left school to take care of your mama, correct?"

"Yes, ma'am."

She reaches over and grabs his hand, giving him a gentle squeeze. "I'm sure she's so proud watching you play for the Rangers from heaven right now."

He blushes and dips his head. "I hope so."

"This is your first year with the team, right?" My father steers the conversation back to football.

"Kind of. I came on mid-season last year."

"He was flagged during try-outs. The team knew they wanted to bring him on the first chance they got." I hate it when Rex sells himself short, as if being on the team is an accident or something. "He's got some untapped running back potential waiting to be used."

Darren snorts. "Isn't it annoying when the number one wide receiver in the league waves his pompoms in the air for you?"

Rex chuckles. "I wouldn't say it's annoying..."

"Bite me," I tell my brother with a big smile on my face.

For the next couple of hours, we watch the game and chat idly about life. My father is retired and tends to his chickens, goats, and whatever other animals he rescues while my mother still works full-time as a contract lawyer. Patrice is an interior designer and takes Rex on a tour of the house after she learns about his newly remodeled kitchen and bathroom.

My father nods his head approvingly when they leave the room. "I like him."

"Yeah, he's pretty amazing." I take Rex's seat while he's out of the room.

"How much longer before the team finds out the two of you are dating?" My father arches his brow, cutting through all the unspoken things to the underlying question at hand.

Darren turns his head in our direction as if to silently ask the same question.

I shrug. "I don't know."

"Are you happy, son?"

From across the room, I lock eyes with Rex talking to Patrice in the living room. He flashes me that coy smile he gives when we catch each other's gaze across the locker room. Unable to resist, my lips spread and I nod. "I really am."

"Then that's all that matters."

After dinner, Rex and I are in the kitchen drying dishes while Patrice and Darren get the kids ready for bed. "I like your family."

"I told you they would love you." I elbow him and then lean forward, planting a kiss on his neck.

"Like you?" he murmurs.

My heart stops for a second. "I didn't mean to freak you out."

"Did you mean it?"

"Of course, I did." I set the platter down and turn toward him, resting my hip against the counter. "I know we've only been seeing each other for a couple of months, but I knew I loved you the moment we kissed."

He presses his lips together. "Growing up with no family other than my mother, I haven't had a lot of practice saying the words out loud."

"You don't have to say them if you aren't ready, Rex." I brush my fingers through his hair and tilt my forehead to his. "It doesn't change how I feel about you."

"I'm going to say it when you least expect it, when it really means something," he whispers more to himself than to me.

"Want to stay for the last game, or do you want to head back to the hotel?"

"Split the difference. We'll stay until halftime and then say our goodbyes."

"Sounds perfect, baby."

An hour and a half later, we are standing at the front door saying our goodbyes.

"Will we be seeing you for Christmas, Rex?" my mom chirps.

I rub the top of my head. "I haven't had a chance to ask him yet, Mama."

"Don't we have a game on Christmas?" Rex looks at me, his brow furrowed.

Tilting my head in Darren's direction, I say, "We both do, which is why we are celebrating a day later in Atlanta."

"You have to come," my mom adds, grabbing both of his hands in hers.

"I—" he glances at me "—would love to."

"Good, then it is settled." She pulls him into her arms and plants a kiss on his cheek. "Take care of my baby."

"Yes, ma'am." He blushes as she steps back.

I roll my eyes at my mama's blatant manipulation and pull her into my arms. "See you in a month."

Darren chucks me on the shoulder and then slaps palms with Rex. "See you guys soon. Be careful out there."

My father walks us to the car. "You fly home tomorrow, yes?"

"We do."

"Okay, well, we will see you at Christmas. You're going to love Dorothy." He shakes Rex's hand and gives me a hug.

Rex waits until we are in the car to ask, "Who is Dorothy?"

"His goat." I chuckle, shaking my head and putting the rental in reverse.

Once we drive out of the neighborhood and hit the main drag, Rex slides his hand into mine. "Thank you for bringing me."

"Thanks for coming."

"Christmas in Atlanta, huh?" His thumb slides soothingly over the back of my hand.

"Yeah." I bring his hand up to my mouth and kiss his fingers. "Stick with me, baby, and I'll show you the world."

Chapter 10
Rex

Feelings I can't express run through me and make every nerve-ending tingle. I'm happy, joyous, and so unbelievably grateful to have Devlin in my life. With him, I feel like I'm finally home. He's the kind of man I strive to be—sweet, caring, loving, open and honest—and he wants to give it all to me.

We walk through the lobby and into the elevator hand-in-hand.

It feels good.

It feels right.

And I want to give him all of me, just like he gives me all of him every day.

I've been thinking about this for weeks, but I was unsure how to approach it until now. With Devlin I need to be direct and honest with what I want and how I feel, just like I believe he would be with me.

We enter our room and I sit on the edge of the bed, watching as he takes off his coat and puts his phone on its charger. He kicks off his shoes and then brings his eyes over to me. "Is everything okay, babe?"

I pat the space next to me. "Come here."

He sits next to me and I bring my knee up to face him. I wrap one hand around his forearm, and the other around his thigh, caressing him gently with a rhythmic swipe of my thumb. "There's something I've been wanting to talk to you about, but I didn't know how to bring it up."

"Okay?" He frowns.

"I've spent my life feeling awkward about sex. With you, I not only enjoy the physicality, but I crave the intimacy you're so good at." I glance down at my hand on his arm. "I'm afraid I take more than I give to you."

Devlin tilts my chin up, forcing my gaze to his. "What are you talking about, baby?"

"If I had more sexual experience, would you be so gentle or patient with me?"

"Am I gentle and patient? I feel like I'm constantly pawing at you."

"I want to experience everything with you—" I lick my lips "—even the things I've never done before."

His lips part, and he nods slowly. "I see."

"Maybe we could try this weekend?"

He cups my face and kisses me with a tenderness that speaks of love and devotion. "Whatever you want, babe."

The next morning, we were blessed with a rare partially sunny day as we walked along the water's edge and through Pier 57. When we get back to Spring City that night, Devlin drops me off at my house and tells me to pack a bag for the weekend. This will be the first time I've been to his house, considering Aggie only moved out last week.

Saturday afternoon, I arrive at his home with a bag of groceries. His house is beautiful. The exterior is slate stone and light gray stucco, the driveway is charcoal cobblestones, and there are wrought iron Juliet balconies adorning every French door. His front double door is an architectural masterpiece of glass, metal, and shiny black wood. The landscape is lush and meticulously maintained.

Honestly, I'm a little embarrassed driving my older Dodge truck onto his street, much less into his pristine garage. Maybe I should have bought that Mini Cooper after all.

"Hey, babe." Devlin greets me with a kiss, wearing a pair of loose-fitting sweatpants and a tight anime T-shirt. How can he make such scrub wear look so damn enticing?

"This house is amazing." I follow him inside, where it is a combination of white granite, chrome and stainless steel fixtures, and rich dark gray leather.

He shrugs. "I bought it like this. I think it's nice, but sterile compared to your house. Who knows, I might have to hire your contractors to bring some warmth into this place. The only room I designed is my game room in the basement. Want to see?"

"Of course." We put the groceries on the counter, and I follow him while he gives me a tour. Confronted with a full wall of glass-encased game pieces, most meticulously painted, I smile and shake my head. "You might be my king, but you are also king of the geeks."

Devlin turns his body into mine, backing me up against a giant wood table. He presses the length of his body against my own, his hands wrapping around my hips as his lips hover over mine. "I'll wear a crown if you want me to."

"That might have to happen." Chuckling, I rub my body against his. "Are you hungry?"

"Starved." He waggles his brow and moans low in his throat.

"I meant for food."

Rolling his eyes, he dramatically sighs and takes a step back. "I can eat."

I brazenly take a step forward and cup him through his sweatpants, enjoying the flirty tease that used to be so foreign to me. "We have all weekend, right?"

He pushes his hips forward and sucks in his breath. "Yes, babe, we do."

"Then let's go eat."

While Devlin's kitchen is luxurious, I think I like my new kitchen more. That might be because I know where everything is, or the pride associated with the recent remodel. Devlin sits on one of the countertops and watches as I food prep, his long legs dangling over the edge, almost like a kid waiting to open his Christmas presents.

Speaking of which...

"If I come with you to Atlanta, I'm going to need help picking out presents for everyone," I say while cutting chicken breasts into bite-sized chunks.

"There is no if, and you don't have to buy my family presents." He shakes his head and takes a sip of his seltzer water. "Hell, I have no idea what to get Darren or Patrice. For my parents and the kids, well, I think it would be better if we gave them their presents as a couple."

I don't know why—I mean, I know how Devlin feels about me, he's been very honest about it—but hearing him call us a couple makes me all misty-eyed. I put down my knife and walk between his splayed knees, leaning forward and planting a chaste kiss on his lips. "So, what are we getting them?"

He wraps his fingers around my head and holds me in place, slipping his tongue into my mouth to kiss me breathlessly. I moan as my entire body wakes up, heeding the call his lovingly erotic touch sends to me.

As soon as I melt into him, he pulls back enough to look me in the eye, his sparkling with mischief. "You are such a sweet man, you know that?"

"And you are a tease."

His grin grows wide. "I love how you sink into me, baby."

"I can't help it. Your kisses are that good." I push back from him and return to prepping our chicken stir-fry. "So? Presents?"

"Patrice took pity on me last year and created an online toy registry for the kids. You and I can look through it later and pick a few things for both of them."

"And your parents?"

He sighs. "I usually buy my dad a bottle of scotch and sign my mother up for some kind of gift of the month thing. One year it was gourmet chocolate strawberries. Another year it was unusual international snacks. I was thinking this year I would donate to one of her favorite charities and maybe have a placard made in her name. It's hard to buy presents for them. Whatever they want, they buy."

I think back to my best Christmas with my mom. I was eleven. She'd taken on a third shift at the diner to scrape up some extra money for presents, and on Christmas Eve took me to Walmart. She had me pick out my favorite brand-name snacks—chips, cookies, and a six-pack of soda—as well as a movie bundle from the metal bin in the middle of the aisle. Of course, she also bought me jeans, two pairs of sneakers, and a handful of graphic T's to get me through the rest of the school year. I knew it wasn't much, but that Christmas it thrilled me to have a fun night at home eating junk food and watching TV with my mom.

I snort and shake my head, immediately regretting the action rife with judgment. "Shit. I'm sorry, Devlin. I didn't mean that."

He bows his head. "I'm sure our Christmases were very different growing up."

"Yeah, but we were both surrounded by love—which is the most important part."

Devlin hops off the counter and wraps his arms around my waist, resting his chin on my shoulder. He loves to hold me like this and I love having him do it. "Do you think your mom would have liked me?"

I glance over my shoulder. "She would have LOVED you."

He rests his forehead between my shoulder blades and holds me for a minute, his touch infusing me with warmth. "Sometimes this feels like a dream, you know?"

I nod but say nothing as I'm still unsure how to verbalize all that I am feeling. It's overwhelming.

He draws in a deep breath and then lets me go, smacking my ass before he walks out of the kitchen. "I'll set the table."

Two hours later, we are relaxing in his game room where he shows me his old DM notebooks and tells me some of the fascinating storylines he created over the years.

"You are very creative."

He shrugs. "Darren and I used to tell each other stories and build on each other's worlds. You know, there was a time our mother didn't think it was safe for us to play football. She thought we had our heads too far in the clouds to protect ourselves."

"Instead, you turned out to be the perfect combination of both—doer and dreamer."

Devlin chuckles, sets his notebook down, and slides his hand on my thigh. "I'm glad you're here."

"Me too."

"Want to take a shower and then watch TV in bed?"

We haven't talked any more about my awkward request from Thursday night, but I can't help but wonder if this is it.

I'm both nervous and excited about crossing this final threshold. I mean, I'm sure it's not the final threshold. No doubt there are all kinds of erotic things to do with your lover that I haven't fathom doing, but I feel like penetration is the last of the average relationship list. Ever since the idea—or question of *will we*—popped into my head, I've felt a deep urge building in my belly. While I want to feel him inside me, just as I crave the pleasure of sliding inside him, I'm more excited about the emotional connection I think sharing this with Devlin will mean to both of us. This isn't something I've fantasized about doing, but with him, I want everything.

I nod shyly. "Yes."

He stands and interlaces his fingers with mine, walking me through the house and up two flights of stairs to his bedroom. Letting go of my hand, he points to his dresser. "I cleaned out all the drawers on the left side, in case you want to bring over more clothes. I want you to feel comfortable coming over whenever you like."

Devlin pulls off his shirt and then gathers up the hem of my polo, pulling it up and over my head. Without words, he wraps his arms around my waist and pulls me into his body, his hands splaying across my back. He kisses me with the kind of sweet possession I've come to crave, once again causing me to melt into him.

He chuckles low in his throat. "Love that."

"I love you." The words come out effortlessly as our eyes lock in meaningful silence.

Smiling, Devlin unbuttons my khakis and pushes them down before stepping out of his sweatpants. "Come with me, baby."

His shower has multiple rain heads hanging from the ceiling with handhelds on either end. The glass walls stretch to the ceiling, and the enclosure fills quickly with steam after Devlin turns on the water. He opens the door and pulls me in behind him, my eyes going to a dildo and a bottle of lube on the tile bench.

Devlin's eyes follow mine. "If you want to try that tonight, I have to prep you. The last thing I want to do is hurt you."

His thoughtfulness and attention to my comfort, which I should expect, touches me deeply. I pick up the dildo and wrap my fingers around it, figuring it to be about half the size of him. Arching my brow, I cast him the unspoken question and he chuckles. "Not a replacement for me, just something to get you started."

"I would say not."

Grabbing the soap off the tray and lathering up my hands, I glance down to find his cock hard and erect. I slide my sudsy hands down his magnificent chest and chiseled abs before fisting his dick and cupping his balls.

Devlin closes his eyes and sucks in his breath, growling softly. "I love how you touch me."

"It's like running my hands over a statue. You are priceless, like a work of art."

"Would you still love me if a had a pot belly?" He reaches down to stroke me. "Because if you keep feeding me like you do, that might happen."

"I'll keep you happy and healthy, my king. I promise." I lift up on my toes when he slides his soapy hand between my legs and presses his finger near my asshole.

"Are you sure you want to do this?" Devlin arches his brow.

"With you—yes."

He kisses me once more and then takes a step back. "Turn around and put one foot up on the bench. Use the wall to brace your hands. I'm going to talk you through this, so you know what I'm doing. Do your best to relax."

I do as he says, excitement rushing through my limbs. The rain head above pours a steady deluge of warm water between my shoulder blades, while Devlin uses his soapy hands to massage my muscles. His cock slides along the crack of my ass with every push of his hips, my dick jumping in anticipation. Then he reaches around and strokes me as his lips trail kisses down my spine. "This might be uncomfortable at first, but if it hurts at all, you tell me. Don't grin and bear it."

"Okay."

He steps back and the water pressure overhead changes to a gentle mist. From behind me, I hear the top of the lube bottle pop open. Then he's touching my asshole with slick fingers, sliding and pushing against the puckered rosette. "I'm going to warm you up with my fingers, and then with the dildo."

A small gasp escapes my lips when he pushes his

fingertip inside me. He uses short strokes at first and then goes a little deeper each time I exhale, my body relaxing with each calming breath. Soon the rhythmic pumping of his finger in my ass has a need building low in my belly, and I push back on him as if to beg for more.

Devlin's lips are on my spine again, his other hand stroking my cock. "That's my prince, taking it so well his first time. Are you ready for more?"

"Yes," I moan as he slips a second finger inside.

"Fuck, it is hot watching you enjoy this." He scrapes his teeth on my shoulder, each stroke of my cock more insistent.

"More," I whimper a minute later, unable to worry about what he might think of me being a needy little brat.

He lets go of me and grabs the dildo off the bench, adding a few more drops of lube to the tip. "Nice and relaxed, Rex."

The foreign sensation has me clenching at first, but I push back as he instructs, and then I'm overrun with pleasure from the top of my head to the tips of my toes.

"Ahhh." I throw my head back, panting, as Devlin slowly works the dildo in and out of my ass.

"How does that feel?" He grips my hips with his big hand and kisses my neck.

"So good." I slap my palm against the wall, a desire to explode tightening up my balls.

"You're doing so well." He reaches around and strokes me again while pressing his thighs against the backs of mine, covering me like a second skin. His hand controls the dildo between us, but it's the gentle roll of his hips that thrusts it in and out of me.

"Devlin, I'm going to come."

"Come for me, baby."

I explode all over the tile bench, my body jerking in Devlin's hands as a heavy load shoots out of my cock. My body shudders, and I'm thankful he told me to brace myself against the wall. Otherwise, I might face plant on the tile floor.

On the other hand, I know Devlin would never let me fall.

That was, by far, the hardest I've ever come in my life, but I know this is only the beginning.

Chapter 11
Devlin

I pull the dildo out of Rex's ass and toss it onto the bench, spinning him around and pushing him back against the tile wall. With my hands bracketing his face, I claim his lips with the ferociousness coursing through my body. Something about being Rex's first makes me territorial and primal, and I want to mark and claim him as mine.

He meets my strength with his own, pushing me down on the tile bench. He drops to his knees and wraps his lips around my cock, licking and sucking with the same kind of primal desperation I feel.

"Let me hear you, my king," Rex growls from between my legs.

Groaning, I thrust my fingers into his hair and tighten my grip, bringing my hips up to fuck Rex's mouth as he sucks, slurps, and strokes me as hard as he can. I know the sound gets him going, and I've found the more turned on he is, the closer to coming I get.

I come without warning, shooting my seed deep down his throat. Rex doesn't hesitate to swallow every drop, the sexually shy guy I first kissed six weeks ago gone. I pull his face up to mine and kiss him hard with all the love I have for him.

He sits back on his heels with his eyes on me, his beautiful body in perfect supplication, and fills his mouth with the water drizzling down on us. Spitting out a mouthful, he grins up at me with something akin to flirty pride. "That was amazing. Now what do we do?"

Chuckling, I lean back on my elbows to catch my breath. "Are you ready for more?"

"Yes."

I help him to his feet and then shut off the water and grab us two towels. As he's wrapping his around his waist, I grab the dildo and the lube out of the shower and bring them into the bedroom with us. Tossing them onto the bed, I playfully push Rex down on his back and then climb on top of him, sliding my hands through his thick hair. "You've been growing it out."

"I have."

"Why?"

"Because you like touching it, and I didn't want to dissuade you." He waggles his brow like he's clever.

"I think you are getting quite good at flirting."

"Think so?" He turns his face into my hand and kisses my palm. "I think you bring it out in me."

"I'm glad I do. How do you feel? Are you sore?" I roll to his side and run my hand over his beautiful body.

He shakes his head. "Not sore, but energized."

To emphasize his point, he flexes his ab muscles and makes his cock jump under the towel.

I lick my lips and peel away the terry cloth covering him. "Are you ready for more?"

"Yes, my king," he growls.

"Mmmm." Wrapping my fingers around him, I lean down and take him in my mouth. "Naughty prince."

It doesn't take me long to have Rex writhing beneath me, one hand gripping my shoulder as I work him into a frenzy. Lifting on my elbows, I move to position myself between his legs, pushing his thighs up so his ass raises off the towel. I slide my tongue across his asshole, rimming his most delicate entrance, before gently sucking his balls into my mouth.

Rex grips the comforter next to his hips, panting his approval as I do it again and again.

When I think he can't take much more, I sit up on my knees and grab a condom and the bottle of lube, waiting for him to lock gazes with me. "Ready, baby?"

"Yes." He's breathless and damn near out of his mind with need—like me.

Tearing the foil packet open with my teeth, I quickly sheath myself and then pop open the top of the lube, dripping a few drops onto his puckered hole. I slide my fingers inside and thoroughly coat him, adding more to myself before lining up the tip of my cock and pushing forward gently. "Like in the shower, if it's too much, you need to let me know."

"It won't be too much." He reaches between our

bodies and wraps his fingers around my forearm. "I need it. I need you."

"You have me, Rex. Forever." I push forward a little more, pumping my hips every half inch until he relaxes and lets me slide in farther.

"Goddamn, you are a lot bigger than the dildo," Rex pants when I'm fully seated inside of him.

Perspiration breaks out on my forehead. "Yeah, and you are so fucking tight."

I slowly slide in and out, dragging the length of my cock across the bundle of nerves until Rex is moaning his pleasure. "Oh, that's so good. You can go faster."

Quickening my thrusts, I fist his cock in unison, desperate to pound my hips into his ass until I release again. But I won't do anything to hurt my prince. He likes a gentler touch, and I'm willing to give him whatever he needs—always.

He wraps his fingers over mine, jerking himself rougher than I thought he liked. "Harder, faster. I want you to come."

His brown eyes are nearly black as he stares up at me and nods his encouragement. I lean forward and kiss his knee, letting go of his dick to use my hands to push his legs up higher. "Touch yourself, baby. Come with me."

I pump my hips harder and faster, growling as need builds in my balls. Rex throws his head back, his mouth open, his breath ragged as his dick spurts a thick, pearly white load onto his stomach. Watching him come with me deep in his ass takes me over the edge as I thrust my hips forward hard, holding still as my cock jerks through my climax.

Gasping for breath, we stare at each other as the full weight of what we've shared settles between us.

"I love you," I say as I sag back on my heels, slipping free from his ass.

Rex lifts on his elbows and looks at me through his splayed knees. "I love you, too."

"I'm going to rinse off. Do you want to come?" I roll to my hip and slide my feet off the bed.

"Yeah."

We rinse and towel off and then slide beneath the covers of my king-sized bed. I pull him into my arms and pepper his face with kisses, using my fingers to caress his jaw. "Thank you."

"For what?" he says sleepily, his eyes fluttering closed.

"For trusting me with your body and your heart."

"You would never hurt me," he murmurs.

"No, I wouldn't." I say nothing else, letting my prince fall to sleep in my arms, but in my head, I wonder if he'll end up hurting me.

Darren was right. I love openly and hard, and I think if Rex changes his mind about me or us at some point, it might kill me.

ost nights we fall asleep with me as the big spoon and Rex as the little spoon, and we usually wake up in the opposite position. This morning I stir with Rex's hand lazily caressing my hip, his hard dick pressing against my ass, and his soft snore reverberating in my ear.

This is new.

I reach back and run my palm over his ass and down the back of his thigh, pulling his leg up over my hip to drape him across my back.

My personal princely blanket.

Rex's soft snore turns into a low, throaty moan when he shifts his hips, grinding his cock against me. "Good morning, my king."

"Mmmm. It certainly feels like a good morning."

"I've woken up with hard-ons before, but never like this."

"Do you want to fuck me, Rex?" I arch my ass into him.

He hisses. "Can I?"

I reach over to the nightstand and grab the towel, condom, and lube from last night. "How do you want me?"

"How do you like it?" His voice is more alert and I know if I roll over to face him, his eyes will be bright and focused.

"I like it just like this." I reach between us and fist him. "Lay me face down with a pillow under my hips and I'm in heaven."

Rex sits up and pushes the blankets off of us. I hear him rip open the foil, his breath shallow as he sheathes himself. Then he's grabbing a pillow and urging me to lift my hips off the mattress. "Do you want one pillow or two?"

"Two." He grabs a second one, propping my ass up in the air and positioning himself between my knees.

Rex runs his hands over my body, caressing my calves and then the cheeks of my ass before draping himself over my back to press kisses against my neck. "Tell me what to do."

"You know what to do, baby." I glance over my shoulder. "Fuck me."

He nods and leans back on his heels, dribbling lube down the crack of my ass. Using his finger, he coats me and then lines himself up, pushing forward gently. I take a deep breath and let it out slowly. Obviously, this isn't my first time, although it has been a while with a partner, so I will myself to relax and give myself and this moment over to my lover.

Rex takes care, every movement thoughtful, until he's fully seated inside of me. He groans, his fingers flexing against my hips, and leans forward to plant sweet kisses against my back. "Is this okay?"

"You feel wonderful." I turn my head to the side and lie my chest flat, my hands near my knees as I arch my back deep and ass high in offering. "Take your pleasure, baby. I promise I will love it."

His gaze is soft, almost dreamy as he pushes and pulls, each stroke sending tingles up my spine and straight to my balls. I pant and moan. The gasps escaping my lips turn him on more, each thrust more insistent as he chases his orgasm.

"Ahhh, I'm going to come." Rex releases with a gentle roar before slumping forward, his hands finding mine on the mattress. He interlaces our fingers and holds onto me with his forehead presses against my back.

"How do you feel?" I squeeze his fingers.

He pulls out and uses the towel to clean me before climbing off the bed to discard the condom in my bathroom. I roll to my side, repositioning the pillows and smile as he slides back into bed beside me. Rex brushes his fingers over my half-hard cock. "Do you want to get off?"

I grab his hand and bring it up to my lips, kissing each fingertip. "Not right now."

"Are you hungry?"

"Always."

"I was thinking I'd whip us up a couple of omelets." He cups my jaw, his gaze searching my face. Is he looking for something, or trying to tell me something?

"That sounds amazing." I kiss the inside of his palm.

"I'm really happy, Devlin." He blushes slightly. "You make me happy."

My heart soars. "Me too, baby. Me too."

Chapter 12
Rex

We spend the day snacking, talking, and snuggling on the couch while bingeing the Shrek movie franchise. I have my head in Devlin's lap, his fingers lazily combing through my hair, when the garage door flies open and Aggie's nearly three hundred pounds of intimidating muscle pushes his way into the house.

"I fucked up," he blurts, his movements erratic, his head swiveling around frantically. His eyes land on us, and I swear he looks like he's on the verge of tears. "Devlin, I don't know what to do."

And then he stops, the air in the room suddenly thick as his eyes widen and he sucks in his breath.

I spring up and push back from Devlin, unsure how our teammate, his best friend, is going to react.

Aggie closes his eyes and turns his back to us, taking a couple of steps toward the door he pushed through seconds ago. "I'm so sorry. I shouldn't have burst into the house. I don't live here anymore and I have no right. I'm so sorry."

Devlin pushes to his feet as Aggie rambles, his eyes coming to me before he takes a few steps toward his best friend. "Yo, man, what's going on?"

Aggie hangs his head. "I'm so sorry."

"Yeah, you've said that." Devlin wraps his hands around the big guy's shoulders and turns him toward me. "Come sit down and tell me what's going on."

He sits in the chair next to the couch and brings his eyes up to me. "Sorry."

I shrug because I'm not sure what to say. We don't know each other well—we've only had one burger together a couple of weeks ago, the day Jepson mouthed off to Deidre Scott—so I'm not sure how he feels about his best friend dating me.

Devlin sits next to me and slides his hand on my back to show solidarity. While his touch comforts me, I'm on edge, waiting for Aggie to disapprove in some subtle way.

His eyes bounce between us. "How long have the two of you been together?"

Devlin speaks for us, which I'm more than thankful for. Honestly, I don't know what I would say at this point. "We started hanging out near the beginning of the season, playing WarCraft online, having dinner and stuff."

He nods, glancing down at his hands. "So that's where you've been at night. You couldn't bring your boyfriend home because my loser ass was camped out in your basement. Why didn't you tell me?"

Devlin sighs. "Because of the teammate thing. We were waiting to see where our relationship headed before telling anyone."

"Even your best friends?"

"Even our best friends."

"Well, your secret is safe with me, and when you decide to go public, you have my support." Aggie locks eyes with Devlin. "I just want you to be happy, man."

"I know you do, and I am happy." Delvin lifts our joined hands to his mouth and kisses it. "Very happy."

I fidget and then push to my feet. "I was just about to start dinner. Want to join us?"

"You cook?" Aggie glances up at me.

"Uh, yeah."

"Me too. I made..." He trails off as a memory hits him.

Devlin stands too and offers Aggie his hand. "Why don't you tell us what's going on? It's not like you to barge into anywhere except a defensive lineman, so what's got you troubled?"

I lead us into the kitchen where Devlin and Aggie sit on barstools on the other side of the island. I grab a couple of seltzer waters out of the refrigerator and slide them across the counter.

Devlin smiles. "Thanks, babe."

Aggie grabs the can and lets out a heavy sigh. "Well, I guess I've been keeping my own secret—one Rex kind of already knows."

Raising my brow, I exchange a look with Devlin, who cocks his eyebrow in surprise. "You already know?"

I shrug. "Maybe."

"Last night, Deidre and I spent the night together."

Devlin's eyes grow wide. "No shit? Does Declan know?"

Aggie's head drops. "He does now. The whole family knows."

"What happened?"

"Ellen attacked us with acid as we exited my building."

As soon as he says this, I noticed the bandage on his hand. "Are you okay?"

Aggie looks at his hand. "Yeah."

"Is Deidre?" Devlin prompts.

"She had to be rushed to the hospital. They let her go an hour later, but only after we got into a huge fight and she kicked me out of her room." He shakes his head. "I don't know what to do. I'm in love with her, but how can I expect someone like her to deal with the shit in my life?"

"Where's Ellen?"

"Jail."

"Good," Devlin nearly snarls, the look on his face pure disgust. "I hate that crazy bitch."

I've only heard rumors, but judging by the look on my lover's face, they are all true. "What did Declan say?"

Aggie shakes his head. "I don't know. I've been avoiding his phone calls all afternoon."

"More importantly, what did Deidre say?" Devlin says in a gentle tone.

"She's angry."

"I think she has a right to be angry, man. She's not the kind of woman to allow a personal attack slide—specifically a physically brutal attack. Is she angry at the situation or you?"

"Both." He runs his hand through his hair. "I don't know. I told her I can't risk her safety, and she called me out for pushing her away for a bullshit reason. We all know I don't deserve someone like her, but I thought I'd worked through that. I was ready to give her everything I have and take anything she will give me, hoping we could build something together. We had an amazing night and started the morning perfectly, then Ellen ruined it and I'm back to questioning my whole existence and self-worth again."

"You're scared," I say from a place of intuition. I might not know Aggie, but I know what it feels like to be scared of being vulnerable and accepting another person's love—filled with the knowledge that you aren't and never will be good enough for them. That's how I feel about Devlin. I'm nowhere near his league and yet he says he loves me.

He looks up and nods. "Yes."

Devlin wraps his hand around the back of Aggie's neck. "Deidre is an amazing woman, Ags. A scary-ass ball-buster to anyone who crosses the people she loves. If there's a chance she loves you too, you can't let her go."

"How do I fix this?"

"Go to her." I shrug. "Tell her you're scared. Be honest about your feelings."

Something in Aggie's brain switches on because his

whole demeanor changes. He nods, checks his watch, and pushes back from the countertop. "I've got to go."

"Are you going after her?" Devlin arches his brow, a wry smile on his beautiful face.

"Yeah."

"Good." Devlin slaps his palm on his back. "Don't take no for an answer."

Aggie stands up and offers me his hand. "Thanks, Rex, and sorry again for barging in. Take care of my best friend."

I blush. "I will."

"See you guys next week."

Devlin tilts his head toward the door and winks at me. "I'm going to walk him out."

"Okay."

I busy myself with pulling salad vegetables out of the refrigerator and chopping them up into bite-sized pieces. Devlin comes back a few minutes later and locks the door behind him, sliding up behind me at the counter to wrap his arms around my waist. "You okay?"

"Yeah. That went better than I expected."

"You expect backlash?"

I shake my head. "Honestly, I don't know what to expect."

"I know my friends have our back, and I'm pretty sure the organization will too, even if they don't want to deal with the inevitable press."

"Do you think we can avoid it?"

"Which part?"

"The press."

He shakes his head. "Not if we win a championship ring, baby. Look at Declan's personal life. They talk about him on every Sunday football sports network because he suddenly has a five-year-old child that he's never acknowledged. Scandalous. And Deacon got his fair share of press coverage when he announced his engagement, and he's not even playing anymore."

I sigh and mutter under my breath because I'm unsure if I want him to hear me. "Tell me it'll be worth it."

Devlin gently turns me around to face him, cupping my face in his large hands. "It'll be worth it. I love you, so fuck anyone who doesn't support us."

"I love you too, but I'd like to stay in our little bubble for as long as possible, if that's okay with you."

He kisses me softly and then lets me go, giving me an almost curt nod as he turns away. "If that's what you want."

I watch him walk out of the kitchen and know I've messed up. He thinks I want to deny my love for him, that maybe it's not strong enough to shout it from the rooftops, but that's not it at all. I'm overwhelmed by the enormity of what I feel for him.

Me? I'm nothing.

I'm nobody.

The press won't give a shit about me, but Devlin could lose more than I think he realizes. Plus, I like our bubble and I don't want external pressures ruining what we have between us.

I finish making the salad and am about to sear the

tuna steak when Devlin comes back into the kitchen, his hands stuffed in his pockets. He stares at me, his beautiful eyes a gray color, and then smiles softly. "I know this is all new for you, so we'll take as long as you need."

"I do love you," I say quietly.

"I know."

Chapter 13
Devlin

It's the week before Christmas, and we've clenched the Division with a win over Tampa. It's been a couple of weeks since Aggie walked in on us and I've grown bolder with Rex. At the beginning of the season, we barely knew each other. Now we can be spotted together at lunch or working out at the fitness center. While there is no PDA, our close friendship has to be obvious to anyone paying attention.

We still drive separate cars to the training facility, even on the mornings that we wake up in each other's arms. This morning we left my house at the same time, but Rex is stopping by his place before heading here.

It's six-thirty when I pull into the mostly empty parking lot to find Declan standing outside his car with his arms crossed over his chest.

I park in the spot next to him. "Hey, man. What are you doing here so early?"

Now that he has a five-year-old, Declan's been

skating into the office seconds before the clock hits seven almost daily, so I'm surprised to see him so early.

"We need to talk."

"Yeah, I noticed this morning you called me half a dozen times last night. What's up?"

Another car pulls in and he tilts his head toward the practice field. "Let's take a walk."

"What the hell is going on?" I follow him around the building.

Declan stops and shoves his hand into his hair. "Fuck it. I'm going to cut straight to the point."

"Please."

"Are you dating Rex Williams?"

"What?" I shake my head. "Yes. Why?"

His jaw drops. "You are? Why didn't you tell me? I'm your best friend."

I sigh and lean my back against the building. "We didn't want to make it public knowledge until we knew where it was going."

"Yeah, but how could you not tell me?" Declan shoves his hands in his pockets and cast his gaze to the ground.

"Are you seriously butt hurt that I didn't tell you about my love life?" I chuckle.

He shrugs. "A little."

"Wait." I realize that I'm not asking the most important question. Could Aggie have told him? I suppose it's possible, but I don't think he would sell me out like that. If anything, he'd encourage the three of us to get together and for me to tell Declan myself. "How do you know?"

"Yeah—" he hedges "—that's the thing. Everyone knows, or if they don't, they will by the end of the day."

"What?" My mind immediately goes to Rex. I need to get to him, tell him, prepare him. "What the fuck?"

"So, here's how it went down. Last night, we had our family dinner. Deacon, Dad, Aggie, and I were hanging out in the living room while Amelia, Danny, Mom, and London were outside in the garden. Deidre came storming in with her phone in her hand and hit me with a, 'Is Devlin Frank dating his teammate?' You know she has Google alerts set up for the entire team, and she got three notifications in the span of ten minutes on you."

"Shit." That means the entire Scott family knows, which means the entire head office knows—but does the team know? "I have to find Rex."

Deacon Scott walks around the corner, as if there is a homing device implanted in my left ass cheek.

"Hey, Devlin." He looks from me to Declan and back to me.

I arch my brow. "Deacon."

"I guess it's true."

Narrowing my eyes, I pin him with a look that says *fuck with me and find out*. I like Deacon, I really do, but they will not make me feel anything other than elated about my relationship with Rex. I'm a grown man, for fuck's sake. And if the organization tries to pull some bullshit with me, I will walk and take their championship ring with me. For Rex, I will walk away from all of it. "Is it a problem?"

Deacon shakes his head. "Not for me, the Scott

family, or the head office. We support you one hundred percent."

"And Rex," I state plainly.

"And Rex." He nods and glances at Declan again. "But we need to go upstairs and talk about how you want to handle this."

"Handle what?" I bark.

"The media, Devlin." Deacon stares into my eyes. "You know how our sister is. Deidre's ready to bury this or make it tomorrow's headline... the choice is yours."

"You could tell her the same thing I did—my personal life is none of their fucking business," Declan grumbles.

I shake my head, a million thoughts running through it. "I've got to talk to Rex. This is a decision we have to make together."

Declan's eyes shift to the parking lot. "It looks like he's talking to Jepson and Jaxson right now."

"Shit." I peek around the concrete wall to see Rex leaning against his truck with his hands in his hair.

The three of us climb out of our hiding place and walk across the parking lot. Rex's eyes grow wide when he sees us, but then they fix on me. I know the minute I get close enough to see his red flushed cheeks that his two friends, our teammates, not only know but have confronted him about it. A protective surge of adrenaline pushes through my veins, and I turn my gaze to Jaxson and then Jepson. "What's going on, guys?"

Rex shakes his head, his eyes bouncing from Declan to Deacon and then back to me. "They know."

"Yeah?" I look Jepson in the eye because, between the

two of them, he's the only one stupid enough to mouth off to me about it. "And?"

"God help any football player that has a problem with it." Jepson's jaw tightens, his blue gaze unwavering.

Jaxson sighs. "At least if I get sucker punched again, this time it'll be worth it."

Deacon groans and pinches the bridge of his nose. "I'd like to make the edict that there will be no fucking fighting on this team, but in this case, I can't."

More cars pull into the parking lot and all of our teammates walk past us with their duffle bags to the locker room. Some of them eye us curiously, but that could easily be because we're standing in a clandestine semi-circle like we're discussing world domination.

Deacon chucks me on the arm. "We need to head upstairs. You too, Rex. Jepson and Jaxson, get to the classroom and keep your mouths shut."

Jepson and Jaxson give Rex a reassuring squeeze on his shoulder and bicep and then hightail it across the parking lot. Even though they say goodbye to me, I ignore them and keep my eyes on Rex. What is he thinking right now? Is he freaking out and ready to run to the hills? Does having the support of his two closest friends make this easier?

Declan offers Rex his hand. "It'll be cool, man. Promise."

Rex shakes it and mumbles, "Thanks."

I glance at my watch and then at Deacon. "We'll meet you up there in a few minutes."

Deacon nods. "Okay."

Once the Scott brothers leave, I walk to the front of Rex's truck and lean my forearms against the hood. It kills me not to pull him into my arms, but that might send him over the edge and I need to give him space. "Tell me what you are thinking, babe."

He shakes his head and brings his brown eyes up. "I don't know what I'm thinking. Part of me is relieved because we no longer have to hide. I know you hated that. And part of me is scared our teammates are going to be assholes."

"I can't promise there won't be assholes out there. Turn on any news outlet and someone is screaming about how they don't agree with how someone else lives their lives. But what I can promise is that I will always pick you first."

"What do you mean?"

"I mean that if it came down to choosing between you and football, I'm picking you."

Rex stares at me for a second, his voice hoarse when he speaks. "You'd give up football for me?"

"In a heartbeat." I reach my hand across the hood, my heart in my throat as I wait for Rex to decide.

He leans against the fender and places his hand on top of mine. "I'm not willing to give you up either."

"Good, baby. That's very good. Let's talk to the head office. We need to decide if we're going public or issuing a resounding *no comment*."

We sit side-by-side in a giant conference room with Deacon. Deidre walks in with her laptop cradled in her arm, her eyes glued to the screen. She grabs a remote and hits a button, a giant screen on the wall flickering to life, and then sets her laptop down.

Only then does she bring her eyes up and flash me a friendly smile. "Hey, Devlin."

Declan is my best friend, which means I've spent time with the Scott family. Not a lot, but more than the average football player on the team. She rarely interacts with the players unless there are media matters to handle. "Deidre."

She looks to Rex. "Nice to see you again, Mr. Williams ."

"Please call me Rex."

"And you can call me Deidre." She taps a key on her laptop as the GM, Mr. Daniel Scott, enters the room.

"Sorry I'm late." He tosses a box of muffins on the table and then offers me his hand. We shake and then he reaches over to shake Rex's hand. "Weird morning, huh?"

"Not the wake-up I was hoping for. I still haven't had my coffee."

"Yeah, well, the organization is here to support you. Obviously, we ask for decorum while at work, just as we expect Deacon to keep his hands to himself when visiting the training facility where London works." Mr. Scott raises his brow at Deidre, who rolls her eyes.

"Here's the tidbit I found after digging last night." Deidre moves her desktop to the big screen. "This woman, not sure who she is, posted this on Twitter last night."

The two hundred and eighty characters read: Sad news for those hoping to nab a date with the elusive Devlin Frank: number one wide receiver, MVP, and openly bisexual footballer. Rumor is he's off the market and in a hot-and-heavy relationship, but who is the lucky guy or girl? How about his teammate? More to come...

"How the hell?" I glance at Rex, who shakes his head and shrugs.

"I have my investigator digging into the account owner right now, but I was able to find a photo of the two of you walking hand-in-hand in Seattle. Otherwise, I found bupkis. Unless you tell me otherwise, I assume this tweet is mostly conjecture, meaning there isn't more out there to find. I can easily bury a photo or two of you holding hands, so you tell me what you want to do about this."

I make eye contact with everyone assembled. "We have your full support?"

Mr. Scott and Deacon nod their heads. Deidre smiles.

Turning to Rex—it kills me not to wrap my arm around him—I flash him a small, hopefully reassuring smile. "What do you think?"

"You're the one they're interested in, Devlin. Not me.

This affects your career way more than it does mine." His head snaps up and he looks at Deacon. "Am I fired?"

"For this?" Deacon almost sounds offended. "God no. We're really happy with your performance this season and can't wait to see what you can do next year."

I risk offending Mr. Scott's decorum decree by wrapping my fingers around Rex's wrist. "You know what I want. I don't want to hide who I am or who I love."

Rex's brown eyes lock onto mine and it's like everyone else disappears. It's just us right now, having this life changing heart-to-heart conversation. "I think we should tell the team and see how they react before we worry about the rest of the world."

The lump I've had in my throat since driving up on Declan in the parking lot goes away. "Then that's what we'll do."

Chapter 14
Rex

Devlin says he'll handle everything as we walk with Deacon into the classroom. Before we got off the elevator, he asked me how the twins had heard about us, and I finally had to tell him that they are dating the charity chick, Maryanne Merryweather, and she also has Google alerts set up on all the players. I'm not sure if Deacon already knew about their relationship, but the way his eyes flashed and jaw tightened tells me I messed up.

But that's a problem for another day.

The three of us walk in and Deacon steps to the front of the room, pausing the playback reels and turning up the lights. He tilts his head to Devlin. "The floor is yours."

Devlin clears his throat, scanning the room and meeting every coach and player in the eye. "Yesterday, a tweet about me hit the net. I'm not sure who saw it, but I want to address the rumors with my teammates before they grow out of control. Most of you know I'm bisexual and have dated men and women since high school. Since the beginning of the season, I've been dating a teammate, Rex Williams. The simple fact is we've been dating for months and it hasn't affected the team one bit. If any of you suspected, you never had the proof or the balls to ask the question or lodge a complaint, so I expect no one should have a complaint now."

I don't know what comes over me, but I take a step forward and grab Devlin's hand to keep mine from shaking. "We're in love. I love Devlin Frank with all my heart and I hope you accept it and we continue to play football like we already do."

My words are met with utter silence, but the only person I care about is the one standing next to me. I squeeze his hand and then let go, my cheeks burning hot as I search his beautiful eyes which are currently a mesmerizing blue-green.

"I hope that was okay," I whisper, so only he hears me.

"It was perfect, babe," he says in an equally low voice.

"Fuck yeah!" Declan claps his hands, quickly joined by Aggie, Jepson, and Jaxson. "I have no problems with who you or anyone on this team dates. As the team captain, an owner, and your quarterback, all I care about is we are healthy, happy, and playing our hearts out. I want every single one of us wearing a championship ring this year, and we can only do that as a cohesive team."

Murmurs of *yes* and *absolutely* rumble through the

room, the players and coaches nodding their heads and flashing us thumbs up and/or smiles.

Deacon uncrosses his arms and walks to Devlin's other side. "At the beginning of this season we issued a gag-order on the team without telling you exactly what it was about. I'm sure there were rumors running rampant, but in the end the point was that we are a team, a family, and we protect our own. The President of Communications, Deidre Scott, will take care of any chatter outside of this organization, but inside it we take care of each other. If you are approached by any media outlet or gossipy little girl at the club, you shut that shit down with a *no comment*. Everyone good?"

Another series of yeses filter through the crowd.

"Great. Let's get back to the reels so we can play this damn Christmas game and go home to our families." Deacon nods to our seats, and just like that, life is back to normal. Devlin and I slap palms, and I shakily walk to my seat in the back next to Jepson and Jaxson.

The twins bump fists with me and then the room darkens once again.

I'm sitting here in a state of disbelief.

What the hell happened?

I came out to my team. I publicly professed my love. And now I'm sitting four rows away from the man I love, unable to kiss his perfect mouth, or have him hold me until my nerves calm down and I feel like me again.

Deacon taps my shoulder and whispers, "Come outside."

In a daze, I follow him into the hallway. Devlin, who

I never saw leave the classroom, holds out his hand and pulls me into the next classroom, the door closing behind us. He wraps his arms around me, pulling me tightly against his chest. We don't speak, but the love radiating through his skin speaks volumes.

He rubs my back and presses his forehead against mine, his green eyes with their gold flecks shimmering with unshed tears. "You said you would tell me you love me when I least expected it, when it really meant something, and although I want to hear *I love you* from your lips every day for the rest of my life, your proclamation to our teammates today means more to me than any championship ring. I love you so much, baby."

"There's one more thing I want to say."

"What is that?"

"This team might be a family but in you I found my home. You are my king, I am your prince, and the cosmic forces that brought us together will make sure nothing tears us apart."

Epilogue

Devlin

U p by ten points with less than forty-seconds on the clock, Declan kneels for the final time while the rest of the team, coaches, families, and fans rush the field as confetti canons pepper the sky. My quarterback hugs me and then Aggie and I embrace as the thrill of our win roars through the crowd.

Things move quickly, the league and the networks rushing the end of the field to set up a stage to announce the MVP and present team leadership with the championship trophy.

But that's for Declan and the rest of the Scott family to deal with.

Me, I'm overrun by maroon jerseys—teammates, coaches, and fans hugging me, clasping my hand, and twirling me around—but I'm looking for one man in particular, the one I want to spend the rest of my life with.

Jepson and Jaxson rush past me and then he's there, the most beautiful man I've ever met.

We rush toward each other and Rex wraps his arms around me in a big bear hug and twirls me around in the air. And then it happens. Caught up in the moment—neither of us thinking it through—we kiss while standing in the middle of the field on national television.

It's not a rated X kiss, but it's certainly not brotherly considering our lips part and tongues touch. We pull back sharply the moment we realize what we've done, but when I look into his eyes, I regret nothing. I want the world to know that I love this man as I take his hand in mine.

Of course, there is a reporter standing by—one not covering the trophy presentation—her slack jaw and wide eyes letting me know that not everyone has heard about our relationship.

She leaves her microphone down by her side as she leans toward us. "So the rumors are true? Devlin Frank fell in love with his teammate?"

If she didn't have a dreamy look in her eye, and a sweet, hopeful smile spreading her lips, I might resent the non-championship related question. "Yeah, it's true."

"That is so great!" She bounces on her toes before she's distracted by the voices in her ear which morph her from approving fan into sports reporter. "Can we do a quick interview about the game?"

"Sure." I nod. Rex attempts to take a step away, but I clamp my fingers around his hand, desperate to keep him near.

He lets me know he isn't going anywhere with a quick squeeze of my hand.

She brings the microphone up and stands beside me, turning to face the camera man. "Devlin, wow, what an amazing game! Two-hundred and eighty-four receiving yards, seventeen receptions, and two touchdowns, you now hold the tenth highest record in the league for best receiving stats in a single game and the number one record in a championship. Obviously you and Declan were touted as the dynamic duo before preseason began, but you were able to keep your synergy going all season long. To what do you contribute your success?"

"Well, I'm lucky because not only am I on a great team with a fantastic quarterback, but many of the players are my best friends, so our communication and trust runs deep on and off the field. My personal success is directly influenced by the love and support I get from my family. I couldn't and wouldn't be here today without all of them." I glance meaningfully at Rex who smiles at me in return.

The reporter grins and dips her head. "What's the plan for the off-season and do you see the Rangers heading into next year with the same dominance?"

"Last year, we were good. This year, we were better. I don't see how we can't continue to dominate with such a young, healthy, and hungry team. Not only do we have a record-breaking offense and defense, but our special teams along with our second-string has performed better than most of the league. We won't be satisfied with one championship ring."

"And your off-season?"

Devlin smiles at me. "I'm going to spend time with my family and the man I love."

This ends the Rangers Football Series, but don't worry, your favorite characters will make cameos in future series set in Spring City, Colorado (most of my books).

Signed paperbacks and bundle discounts are available here.
Subscribe to the Witty, Wicked & Wild Community for early access and more.

Also by Kameron Claire

Want more **Witty** Tongues, **Wicked** Needs, & **Wild** Deeds?

Hollywood Lights (Pre-Order)

** Billionaire Romance **

Show Time (Securing Selyne)

Money Shot

Three Shot

Martini Shot

Long Shot

Veteran K9 Team

** Military Romance **

Mine to Cherish

Mine to Crave

Mine to Possess

Mine to Adore

Mine to Covet

Mine to Worship

Mine to Protect

Mine to Treasure

Hot Nights with the Boss

** Forbidden Office / Age-Gap Romances **

Dating the Boss

Flirting with the Boss

Teasing the Boss

Tempting the Boss

Rangers Football

** Sports Romance **

Play Action Fake

Quarterback Sneak

Personal Foul

Two-Point Conversion

Red Zone

Man to Man Coverage

Short Story Collections and Bundles

Animal Attraction 4-Story Collection

Vegas Nights 4-Story Collection

Last Stand Saloon 4-Story Collection

Instalove Bundle

About the Author

USA Today Bestselling Author Kameron Claire writes stories with witty tongues, wicked needs, and wild deeds. Her books emphasize strong female leads and the protective alpha males who know how to love and support kick-ass, take-charge women. Many of her books contain military veterans, boss babes, gentle but dominant men, and goofy K9 hijinks.

Find her everywhere via linktr.ee/kameronclaire
Signed Paperbacks and discounted eBook bundles are available exclusively on her store
Subscribe to the Witty, Wicked & Wild community and read all her books online for as little as $5 a month.